COLT on CHRISTMAS EVE

Ben M. Baglio

Illustrations by Ann Baum

Cover illustration by
Mary Ann Lasher

AN
APPLE
PAPERBACK

SCHOLASTIC INC.

New York Toronto London Auckland Sydney
Mexico City New Delhi Hong Kong Buenos Aires

Special thanks to Lucy Courtenay

0-439-77522-1

12 11 10 9 8 7 6 5 4 3   6 7 8 9 10/0

Printed in the U.S.A.   40
First Scholastic printing, November 2005

One

Mandy Hope pulled her fingers out of her ears. "Are you done yet, Mom?" she asked.

Emily Hope turned around in the passenger seat of the Land Rover and wagged a finger at her. "I've just started," she warned, and opened her mouth to sing again.

"No!" Mandy laughed. "Dad, tell her! No more singing!"

Adam Hope kept his eyes on the road. "Since when could I tell your mother what to do?" he joked. "Come on, Mandy — it's Christmas! You're supposed to sing along to carols on the radio. Anyway, your mother's voice isn't that bad."

"Yes, it is," Dr. Emily said, and sighed. "I sound like a goose."

Mandy leaned forward and rested her chin on her mother's shoulder. "Never mind, Mom," she said consolingly. "Geese aren't supposed to sing. They're talented in other areas."

"Like laying eggs," Dr. Adam said helpfully. "And filling quilts." He turned up the radio and broke into a clear, booming tenor voice: "Jingle bells, jingle bells, jingle all the way . . ."

"Show-off!" Mandy teased, prodding her father in the shoulder. "Great-Aunt Pip will have you singing a solo in the Woodhurst carol service before you know it."

The little town of Woodhurst lay deep in the New Forest on the south coast of England. Mandy flicked through the guide book on her knee to remind herself of the facts she had learned so far about this unique, heavily wooded stretch of land. It extended for one hundred and fifty square miles between the cities of Southampton and Bournemouth, and with just a hundred thousand people living within the bounds of the Forest, it was going to seem pretty empty compared with the rest of England! The ancient trees and pretty harborside villages made it a popular tourist destination, but Mandy had a special connection with the Forest that made her watch out for the first sign of woodland with extra eagerness. Her mom's family had lived in the New Forest for many generations, and for the first time, Mandy and her parents were going to spend Christmas with Dr. Emily's elderly aunt.

Although Mandy had never met her Great-Aunt Pip, she felt sure she was going to like her. The affectionate, knowledgeable way Pip wrote about the animals of the New Forest — especially the wild ponies — in her Christmas and birthday cards proved that they were going to have plenty in common!

Mandy's stomach growled. Her takeout cheese-and-tomato sandwich was starting to feel like a distant memory. Shifting around in her seat, she peered out the car window. *Still no sign of the Forest*, she thought with a sigh. They hadn't stopped since the gas station somewhere near London, and that was almost two hours ago. Compared with the high, dramatic moors and dales of Yorkshire, where Mandy lived with her parents at the Animal Ark veterinary clinic, the countryside here was much flatter, dusted with heather and gorse and the occasional clump of trees. As the winter light began to fade, Mandy could just see the bare tops of trees in the distance, silhouetted against the darkening sky. *Maybe that's the start of the New Forest*, she thought hopefully.

Suddenly, her attention was drawn to a group of three ponies standing together on a scrubby patch of open land. There was no sign of a fence, and Mandy watched with growing alarm as the ponies ambled closer to the road.

"Dad, Mom, look!" She pointed out the window. "Those ponies must have escaped from somewhere."

Emily and Adam Hope exchanged a smile.

"There's nothing funny about ponies running loose," Mandy said indignantly.

"We're in the New Forest," Dr. Adam told her. "You should expect to see wild ponies."

Mandy's eyes widened. "*This* is the New Forest?"

She stared out the window at the rolling heathland and vast, open sky. This wasn't what she had been expecting at all! Ever since Great-Aunt Pip had invited them to stay for Christmas, Mandy had imagined a vast tangle of trees where the sky could only be seen in small blue patches, like something out of a fairy tale.

"The word 'forest' just meant 'hunting ground' in the Middle Ages," Dr. Emily explained. "William the Conqueror hunted here."

"So there aren't any trees?" Mandy asked, disappointed.

"Oh, there are plenty of trees deeper in the Forest," her father corrected. "And plenty of open heathland, too, thanks to the felling of trees for timber in the old days. The New Forest has supplied wood for ships and houses through the ages, you know."

Mandy gazed at the little group of ponies, already just brownish smudges against the heather. To her relief, they were wandering away from the road. She wished she'd looked more closely at them. The wild ponies of the New Forest were the main reason she was so excited to be visiting Great-Aunt Pip. *Still*, she told herself, *we're here for a week. Plenty of time to see more of them.*

"Does anyone own the ponies?" she asked curiously. "Or do they just run around, like deer?"

"The people of the New Forest own them, although they are still mostly wild," her mother explained.

Mandy frowned. "That doesn't make sense."

"Plenty about the New Forest seems a little unusual unless you've lived here all your life." Her mother smiled. "The Forest is governed by ancient rights and traditions stretching back a thousand years. Owning the wild ponies is one of those traditions. There are special breeding programs, even though it might seem as if the ponies roam wherever they want. Pip will tell us more, I'm sure."

"When did you last see Great-Aunt Pip, Mom?" Mandy asked.

"A very long time ago," Dr. Emily admitted. "She's a lot older than my father, who was her little brother, and he was closer to his other sisters. It was so kind of her to invite us to stay. We can all really get to know one another at last."

"It'll be strange not being at home for Christmas," Mandy said thoughtfully. She always spent a lot of time over the holidays with the sick and injured animals in the residential unit at the clinic, cheering them up with Christmas treats and cuddles.

"Only a couple of animals will be staying in the unit over Christmas," Dr. Adam said, as if he could read Mandy's mind. "Simon should have plenty of time to enjoy his turkey and presents."

Simon was Animal Ark's veterinary nurse. He was going to be staying in the Hopes' cottage while they were away. He was wonderful with the sick animals, and Mandy relaxed a little, knowing that the clinic's patients were in good hands.

"Here are your trees, Mandy," said Dr. Emily, jolting her out of her reverie.

Looking eagerly out the window, Mandy saw huge

trees along both sides of the road, tall and stately as soldiers, their rough brown bark covered in ivy and lichen. *Oak trees*, she guessed, tipping her head back to admire the branches that tangled together high overhead. It was too dark to see much beyond the trunks, but Mandy could make out dark green holly bushes and the slim outline of beech trees deeper in the forest. A pair of eyes, illuminated by the headlights, flashed on the roadside, and she saw a rabbit shoot into the undergrowth with a flick of its white tail. Then, with a thrill, she saw a pair of ponies standing head to tail among the trees, looking warm and comfortable in their shaggy winter coats. They were about thirteen hands high, with the broad faces and short, stocky bodies she had seen in photos of New Forest ponies. In the dark, it was hard to tell what color their coats were, but Mandy guessed they'd be dun or bay, the most common colors for Forest ponies.

"We should be able to turn off any minute now," said Dr. Emily, studying the hand-drawn map in her lap. "There should be a white gate next to a mailbox — there!"

The Land Rover crunched up a narrow gravel driveway littered with old leaves and twigs. After two sharp bends, the twinkling lights of Beech End Cottage came into view. Mandy stared, enchanted, at the uneven-looking house of dark red brick. It had a mossy thatched roof and white-framed windows. Dark green ivy and crimson Virginia creeper covered the walls, and a warm yellow light shone out of the windows. Smoke twirled into the evening sky from a pair of chimneys that looked like they were leaning distinctly to one side, and a large gray cat was sitting on the doorstep, its long, plumy tail wrapped around itself like a fluffy winter scarf.

It looked like the perfect witch's cottage, and when a tall, angular-looking woman with short gray-red hair came out of the front door, Mandy wasn't sure whether to be relieved or disappointed that Great-Aunt Pip wasn't wearing a pointed black hat.

"Come in from the cold!" Her great-aunt hugged them in turn and ushered them into the tiny hallway where she could examine them more clearly under the light. "Hello, Emily, dear," she said, giving Mandy's mother a resounding kiss on the cheek. "Skinny as ever, I see. How was the trip? It must have taken you hours. Out of the way, Pyramus," she scolded the gray cat that was winding around her ankles and meowing hopefully.

"He's gorgeous!" Mandy exclaimed, bending down and sinking her fingers into Pyramus's cloudy gray fur. The cat purred and blinked its wide yellow eyes at her.

Great-Aunt Pip laughed. "He's not bad," she said fondly. "Though when he brings half-dead birds inside,

I have a different opinion of him. Come into the kitchen — I have hot soup waiting."

Straightening up, Mandy got the shock of her life as she came face-to-face with a huge barn owl with spreading snow-white wings that appeared to be swooping down on her.

"I must apologize for Twit," Great-Aunt Pip said, seeing Mandy's face. "He dates from a time when it was quite normal to stuff wild animals and hang them on the walls. An awful lot here at Beech End Cottage dates from

long ago." She waved around the dim hallway, where
Mandy could make out more strange animal shapes.
"They've been here longer than I have," she added with
a smile.

Mandy spotted a fox's head above the front door and
a pair of antlers beside it. Old photographs and newspa-
per clippings crowded the walls in dusty picture frames,
while at the far end of the hallway a collection of old
tools hung from pegs. Oddest of all, a badger stood in a
long glass case, one paw raised and its strong, blunt
head tilted to one side. It was all a little creepy, Mandy
decided with a shiver.

In contrast, Great-Aunt Pip's kitchen was bright and
warm, with bright red walls and a pot of what smelled
like mushroom soup bubbling on the cream-colored
stove. Traveler's joy was twisted around the beams on
the ceiling; the fluffy seedpods hung like little lanterns
above the scrubbed oak table where three bowls, some
butter, and a basket of poppy-seed bread stood waiting
for them. Pyramus the cat brushed past Mandy's ankles
and settled down on a flat cushion next to the stove.

"I want to hear everything," Great-Aunt Pip declared
as Mandy and her parents helped themselves to the
food. "How is the clinic? Busy at this time of year, I
expect. Was there snow when you left Welford? Tim
Savage — he's a neighbor of mine, an Agister — thinks

we may have snow in the New Forest this year. If we do, it will be most unusual."

"What's an Agister?" Mandy interrupted, hastily swallowing her mouthful of bread.

"A forest official," her great-aunt replied. "Henry, my late husband, was an Agister, too, and my father was a Verderer." She laughed at the mystified faces around the table. "The New Forest has a lot of old traditions," she told them, "and official posts to go with them. A Verderer is a local judge, so my father was a fairly important person within the area. I'll introduce you to the Savages tomorrow. They have a daughter about your age, Mandy."

The mushroom soup was creamy and delicious, the bread crusty and warm. Mandy crunched on poppy seeds while her parents and her great-aunt talked, and she clicked her fingers quietly under the table. After a moment, she was rewarded by the feel of Pyramus's soft head pushing against her hand, a purr rumbling up from deep in his throat.

After supper, Great-Aunt Pip took them back into the hallway. This time, Mandy was prepared for Twit the owl and decided that perhaps he wasn't so creepy after all.

"This is my late husband, Henry, and the other three Agisters," Great-Aunt Pip explained, taking down a photograph that showed four men wearing thigh-length jackets, jodhpurs, and riding boots. "That's Tim Savage there," she said, pointing to a tall, dark-haired man standing to the left in the picture. "The New Forest is divided into four districts, and each Agister takes charge of a district."

"What exactly does an Agister do?" Dr. Adam asked with interest, examining the photograph.

"Among other things, they supervise the welfare of the ponies," Great-Aunt Pip replied. "They make sure they're healthy and looked after, particularly in the winter."

Mandy had never thought there could be a more perfect job than being a vet, but Great-Aunt Pip made the life of an Agister sound like heaven. She felt a thrill of delight at the thought of spending every day riding around the Forest looking after ponies. Hopefully, she'd meet Mr. Savage, so she could ask him about his job. Even better — maybe she'd get to ride one of the ponies!

"We saw some ponies on the way here," she told her great-aunt as they moved into the living room where a log fire was burning merrily. "They get very close to the road, don't they?"

Great-Aunt Pip made a face. "Unfortunately, they do, yes," she said. "All we can do is warn drivers over and over to watch their speed. And then we hope the ponies have more sense than to wander onto the roads. The trouble is, they see so much traffic that they aren't scared of road noise like other ponies might be, which makes it too easy for them to get into trouble."

Pyramus had followed Mandy into the living room and now jumped onto her lap, curling around several times before settling down. Mandy leaned back in the armchair, stroking the cat's velvety gray fur and listening to her parents and Great-Aunt Pip talking about the past. It wasn't long before her eyelids began to droop.

"Time for bed, Mandy," her mother said.

Mandy quickly opened her eyes. "I'm fine, Mom," she replied. "I'm just . . . really . . . comfortable." She gave a huge yawn, and her mom laughed. "OK, maybe bed would be good," Mandy conceded.

Mandy's bedroom was painted a pretty duck-egg blue and was tucked under the eaves at the back of the house. Feeling the wall to the left of the door, Mandy was surprised to find that it was warm.

"You're right above the living room, so you share a wall with the chimney," Great-Aunt Pip explained. "You should be nice and cozy. Your parents are just down the hall, and the bathroom is downstairs behind the kitchen. Sleep well, and we'll see you in the morning."

When her great-aunt had gone, Mandy walked over to the window and pushed aside the curtain to stare into the forest. Everything was dark and still. She wriggled into her pajamas and brushed her teeth at the sink in the corner of the room. Then she hopped into bed, where her toes found a hot water bottle waiting for her. Settling down, she closed her eyes as the soft sound of a hooting owl floated into the room on the moonlight. *Perhaps Twit comes back to life at night and hunts in the forest,* she thought sleepily, drifting off into warm, woody dreams full of thundering ponies.

Two

For the first few seconds of the morning, Mandy didn't know where she was. She sat up and rubbed her eyes. Dappled light was pouring through her window, and the thin fabric of the curtains cast strange shadows on the uneven walls. When she remembered, she threw back the quilt with a thrill of excitement. They were in the New Forest, and Christmas was only a few days away!

After pulling back the curtains, Mandy splashed some cold water on her face and dragged on her jeans and a fleecy hooded top. Sitting on the end of her bed and pulling on her socks, she stared at the view out her window. There was a large redbrick house on the far side of a field right in front of her, but it was the only house she could see. Mandy looked for ponies, but the pasture was empty. An overnight frost had swirled glittering patterns on the woodland that bordered the field and the other three sides of Great-Aunt Pip's yard. Mandy let her eyes drift over the sturdy oaks and the elegant gray trunks of beech trees; she recognized birches, too, with their delicate branches and silvery stems, and shiny green holly bushes smothered with festive red berries. The trees stood knee-deep in russet ferns, yellow-gold moss, and leaf mold the color of chocolate. Set against a deep blue sky, everything was surprisingly colorful for the middle of winter.

The smell of oatmeal floated into her room, and Mandy suddenly felt ravenously hungry. She flew down the stairs with such speed that she almost fell over Pyramus, who was stretched out on the third step from the bottom. Nimbly pulling her feet up just in time, Mandy leaped over the cat and landed with a thud on the rug in the hall.

"That was quite an entrance," Dr. Adam remarked, looking quizzically at his daughter.

Mandy grinned and bent down to ruffle Pyramus between the ears. "Morning, Dad," she said.

Dr. Adam beckoned her over. "Come here," he said, pointing at the photograph by the front door that he had been examining. "Do you recognize this woman?"

Mandy stared curiously at the photograph, which showed a group of people in tweed jackets and hats, sitting in two neat rows in a forest glade. There were several women in the picture, and from their dresses Mandy guessed that the photograph had been taken early in the twentieth century. She looked closer.

"It's Mom!" She gasped. A cold shiver ran down her spine as she stared at the familiar, neat-figured woman sitting in the middle of the picture.

Dr. Adam beamed. "I thought you might say that," he said. "The likeness is amazing, isn't it? I think this is a photograph of the Verderers and Agisters of the time, with their wives. So that's probably Great-Aunt Pip's grandmother, and therefore your mom's great-grandmother."

As Mandy stared at the photo, she felt a strange rush of connection with the New Forest. Her mother's family had come from here, and they'd probably been here for hundreds of years. Although she was adopted, Mandy knew she was part of this amazing chain of history, too. Like her mother, she belonged in this beautiful place with its wild ponies and unique traditions.

In the kitchen, Mandy's mother and Great-Aunt Pip were sitting at the table clutching steaming mugs of coffee. Mandy served some oatmeal for her and her dad, sat down next to her mom, and reached for the cream and sugar.

"What are you going to do today?" Great-Aunt Pip inquired.

"We haven't decided yet," Dr. Emily said. "But knowing Mandy, she'll want to do something with the ponies."

"I'd like to go for a ride," Mandy said, dreamily imagining the crackle of the frosty ground underneath a pony's hooves.

"Well," her great-aunt began.

They all turned when they heard a knock on the kitchen door. A small, brown-haired girl about Mandy's age popped her head around the door. She had dark, wide-spaced eyes, a snub nose, and a freckled, rosy-cheeked face and reminded Mandy of a woodland creature — a field mouse, perhaps, or a porcupine without its quills.

"I was just about to tell my great-niece about you, Lizzie, dear!" Great-Aunt Pip exclaimed, standing up. "This is Lizzie Savage," she explained to Mandy and her parents. "Lizzie's father, Tim, is the Agister I was telling you about yesterday. They live just over there, in Clearfield Cottage." She pointed out the kitchen window at the house on the other side of the field below Mandy's bedroom window. "Lizzie's the same age as you, Mandy, and completely pony-crazy."

Lizzie Savage looked down at the table, her freckles

almost disappearing as she blushed. She didn't say anything to Mandy but hurriedly pushed a card and a small,
brightly wrapped box across the table to Great-Aunt
Pip. "Mom sent you these," she said shyly. "As an early
Christmas present."

"Thank you!" said Great-Aunt Pip. She unwrapped
the gift and showed Mandy and her parents a pretty
silver box containing some pale green, pine-scented
candles.

"They're lovely, Lizzie." Great-Aunt Pip smiled. "Please
thank your mother for me." She turned to Mandy's
mother. "Lizzie's mother, Helen, works in a local art gallery," she explained. "They have lovely gifts in there.
You must go and take a look."

"Christmas shopping!" Dr. Emily looked at Mandy's
dad. "Adam, let's go over there today. I still have to get
a few things."

"Sounds good to me," he said. "Do you want to come,
Mandy?"

"I'll be fine here," Mandy assured him. She wondered
if she'd be allowed to go for a walk on her own. She
wanted to see some more ponies!

As if reading Mandy's mind, Great-Aunt Pip said, "If
it's ponies you're after today, Mandy, Lizzie can introduce you to a few."

Lizzie looked alarmed and took a step toward the

door, as if she wanted to melt back into the Forest without anyone noticing.

"Lizzie keeps two ponies for riding," Great-Aunt Pip continued. "Perhaps she could take you out to see them, Mandy."

"Really?" Mandy gasped. "I'd love that. Where do you keep them? I saw your field from my window this morning, but it was empty." She paused, noticing the expression on the girl's freckled face. "I mean, I'd love to see them if that's OK with you," she said politely.

"I'm sure Lizzie won't mind," said Great-Aunt Pip. "It'll be nice for her to have company her own age. There aren't many girls your age in this part of the Forest. The ponies are in their other field at the moment, so it'll be a nice walk through the Forest for you."

Sneaking another glance at the still silent Lizzie, Mandy felt awkward. Lizzie wasn't nearly as enthusiastic about the plans as her great-aunt was. "I think —" she began.

"That's settled, then," Great-Aunt Pip said with a smile, reaching for her old waterproof jacket that hung on a nail beside the door. "We're off to the gallery. Enjoy yourselves, and we'll see you back here for lunch."

*   *   *

"Sorry about that," Mandy said, pulling on her jacket and cramming her hat over her ears as she hurried after Lizzie down the path that led away from Beech End Cottage. "I hope it's really OK for me to come. I don't want to get in the way or anything."

Lizzie shrugged, looking even more like a woodland creature in her brown coat. "Whatever," she said quietly. "I don't mind."

Mandy glanced up at the trees arching over their heads. Even without leaves they were magnificent, their trunks wide and stately and their branches woven together like a blanket of rusts and browns, embroidered with blue where the sky peeped through.

"I know what it's like," she tried again, picking her way around the trees and trying to keep up. "Being told to make friends with someone."

Lizzie just blinked and quickened her pace. Mandy got the strong impression that she was trying to lose her. It would be easy to do, she realized, watching Lizzie's fast-disappearing back. Sudden thoughts of Hansel and Gretel losing their way in the witch's forest came to mind, and Mandy lengthened her stride, revising her opinion of Lizzie looking like a porcupine with no quills. Right now, the quills were clearly present.

"What are your ponies named?" she ventured, hopping

over a twisted oak root that looked like a serpent rising out of the brown, leaf-strewn forest floor.

"Quince and Piper," said Lizzie after a pause.

Mandy beamed, imagining two bright-eyed ponies with shaggy manes. "You are so lucky to have ponies. I can't have any animals of my own because I'm too busy helping out at the clinic, but I go riding at a local stable sometimes."

For a moment, Lizzie looked like she might say something. Then she appeared to change her mind, tucking her chin back into the collar of her coat and walking on through the trees. Suppressing a sigh, Mandy followed her. Perhaps she would be more talkative when they reached the ponies.

The New Forest was alive with sound and movement. If it wasn't the wind shivering through the branches, it was a puff of gray fur as a squirrel raced along a branch, or a rustle of frosty leaves at the base of a tree as a wood mouse rushed away. A few birds were singing high overhead as Mandy turned her face to the sky and breathed in the damp, leafy smell of the winter woodland. Even though she was a long way from Welford and the Yorkshire moors, she felt at home.

A sudden flash of movement in the undergrowth caught her eye, and for a brief second she saw the twitch of a fox's brush disappearing behind a large oak tree. Mandy peered around the tree, trying to make as little noise as possible.

The vixen froze in her tracks and glared over her shoulder at Mandy with fierce yellow eyes before making a dash for a hazel copse. Within moments, the slim russet-coated animal had disappeared from sight.

For a moment, Mandy had forgotten about Lizzie. Now, with a sudden prickling feeling between her shoulders, she glanced around for her companion. But Lizzie Savage was nowhere to be seen. Mandy stared at the tree trunks that surrounded her. Where was Lizzie? And for that matter, where was she herself? She wasn't sure whether Beech End Cottage was behind her or off to one side. Trying to control a mounting sense of panic, Mandy took a deep breath and started to retrace her steps, looking for the path.

A gentle whickering sound stopped her in her tracks. A round-bellied gray pony was standing in front of her, glancing inquiringly in her direction. Beside the gray stood a long-legged colt whose coat was a creamy reddish color. The colt tossed his head and whinnied nervously as he retreated behind his mother. Mandy stared at them in delight. Wild ponies!

"The gray one's Willow." Lizzie stepped out from

behind an oak tree and scratched Willow gently between the shoulders. The gray mare whickered again and turned her head to look at Lizzie. Mandy gulped. There was terrible scarring down the side of the pony's face, and a sunken, furred-over place where her eye should have been.

"What happened to her face?" Mandy said, gasping.

Lizzie met Mandy's eyes for the first time. "Road accident," she said. "It was a few years ago. Willow was lucky to survive."

She moved her hand up to tickle Willow behind the ears. The girl seemed like a different person all of a sudden, as if the ponies made her less shy. Mandy glanced at the colt, who was stepping from side to side, holding his catkinlike tail up high.

"That's Jingle," Lizzie said. "Willow's pretty tame if you approach on her good side. Jingle isn't so used to people, so he keeps his distance."

"Why's he named Jingle?" Mandy asked.

Lizzie smiled. "Blind ponies can lose their foals very easily," she explained. "My dad put a bell around Jingle's neck so that Willow could hear him if he wandered off. He doesn't wear the bell anymore, but the name stuck."

Mandy made a soothing noise in her throat to reassure the anxious young horse. Jingle flared his nostrils, watching her all the time with his big, dark brown eyes.

Mandy thought he was the most gorgeous creature she'd ever seen!

"Come on," said Lizzie, giving Willow a final scratch under her whiskery chin. "The field is ten minutes away."

She walked back toward the path with her head bent and her hands in her pockets. Mandy followed her, determined not to get lost a second time.

After a couple of minutes, she sensed that they were being followed. She stopped and looked over her shoulder. "Look," she said. "We've still got company."

A little farther down the path Willow had stopped as well, Jingle close by her side. Mandy grinned. It was like a game of follow the leader.

"They're just curious," Lizzie said.

"They've never seen anything as weird as me, huh?" Mandy joked.

It was the first time Mandy had heard Lizzie laugh. Encouraged, she started walking again, stepping over a mossy log and skirting a dark puddle of freezing water. "Is Willow OK with just one eye?" she asked. "Don't you worry about her having another road accident if she can't see where she's going?"

There was a sudden *whoosh* directly ahead of them, and Mandy's heart jumped into her throat as a car pelted past in a rush of air and noise. The trees had completely hidden a narrow road from view. Behind Mandy, Willow pricked up her ears and stood stock-still until the car's buzzing engine was far away.

"Obviously," Lizzie said with a grin, "humans with good vision can be surprised by New Forest roads, too, if they don't know where they're going. Willow's pretty canny. She listens for the traffic and knows where most of the roads are. We just have to hope that people drive sensibly."

"That driver didn't look very sensible," Mandy muttered, her heart still jumping around like a Ping-Pong ball.

Lizzie looked sad. "It's not unusual to see people going way too fast," she said. She frowned so deeply that her eyebrows almost met in the middle. "There are signs everywhere, but drivers ignore them."

Somewhere deep in the woods, Mandy heard the buzzing of a chainsaw. Willow twitched her ears again before deciding the sound was nothing to worry about. She began to head toward a patch of thick grass at the edge of the road.

"There's another car coming," Mandy said, shading her eyes and peering at the shiny shape that was drawing closer.

"Mandy, get Willow away from the road," Lizzie said, suddenly sounding urgent. "She hasn't heard the car — just the chainsaw. You're nearer. Can you reach her?"

Everything around Mandy seemed to be happening in slow motion. She felt as if she were walking through thick molasses as she watched the gray pony move closer to the road, her blind eye facing the oncoming car. With a gasp, Mandy gave herself a shake. She had to do something — fast! Willow wasn't wearing a bridle, and Mandy didn't want to startle her by grabbing her mane. Bending down quickly, she grabbed a handful of grass and held it out to the pony, using her most persuasive voice. "Nice juicy grass, Willow," she said, holding it out. "Come over here, there's a good girl."

The car seemed to be zooming toward them faster than an airplane. Mandy backed away, trying not to startle Willow by how scared she was. *Come on!* she thought desperately. *Move!*

Three

After what felt like forever, Willow brought her head up and looked at Mandy, blowing air softly out of her nostrils. It was Jingle that made the first move, stepping hesitantly toward the handful of grass as Mandy backed away into the safety of the trees. A moment later, Willow followed.

It wasn't a moment too soon. The car roared past, making Jingle skitter sideways on his endless legs. Willow hardly seemed to notice. She stretched out her neck to take the grass from Mandy's hand and chewed it, looking content.

Lizzie's face was white. "Thanks," she muttered. "She

probably would have been OK, but . . . thanks." She set off along the shoulder of the road with her hands thrust in her pockets once more.

Following her, Mandy watched the quickly disappearing car and felt a jolt of anger. Why were drivers so careless in the Forest? Didn't they realize there were wild ponies nearby that could be hurt?

She was thinking so hard about the speeding driver that the sudden appearance of an iron gate and an open field at the side of the road took her by surprise. Trees grew close on three sides, but there was a small group of new-looking houses on the farthest side of the field.

Three ponies were grazing quietly side by side in the middle of the pasture. They were built like Willow and Jingle, small and stocky, but they looked as if they were regularly groomed, with glossy coats and less matted manes and tails.

"Do you mind waiting here?" Lizzie looked awkward. "It's just that they aren't used to you."

"Fine." Mandy rested her chin on the gate and watched as Lizzie hurried over to the ponies. There was a gray, a dark bay, and a skittish skewbald that kicked up its legs and raced around the field a couple of times before skidding to a halt right in front of Lizzie.

Mandy watched as Lizzie pulled a roll of mints

from her pocket and fed them to the ponies as they nudged her, whickering quietly. Lizzie leaned close to all three ponies and whispered in their ears before feeding them a few more mints.

"Can I come and say hello?" Mandy called.

Lizzie looked thoughtfully at her. "OK," she said at last, "as long as you're careful. Keep your voice low. Don't do anything that might startle them."

Mandy resisted the urge to point out that she knew how to handle horses. Lizzie didn't know much about her, and Mandy guessed that the shy, brown-haired girl was just being careful. Mandy couldn't really do anything but approve — she wouldn't want anyone to scare the ponies, either. She walked across the field, feeling the mud suck at her boots — not surprising for the time of year, she supposed. When she reached Lizzie and the ponies, Mandy stretched out her hand very slowly toward the bay's chocolate-colored nose.

"That's Quince," said Lizzie, holding onto the skewbald and stroking his thick brown-and-white mane. "She's very gentle. Piper here is a bit wild, as you probably saw."

Mandy glanced at the little gray, who was standing farther back, watching them.

"That one's Puffin," Lizzie added. "He's Dad's."

Mandy looked at the gray pony with surprise. He was barely fourteen hands high. "You mean your dad rides him?" she asked dubiously. "He's very small to take a grown-up on his back."

"Dad rides Quince, too. New Forest ponies are tougher than they look," Lizzie said, resting her face against Piper's whiskery cheek. "Back in the sixteenth century, King Henry the Eighth released some of his battle stallions into the New Forest to breed with the native ponies and produce a horse that would have lots of stamina and strength. This was the result." She gazed fondly at the stocky ponies grouped around her.

"So all the wild ponies in the Forest are related to royalty?" Mandy asked, impressed.

Lizzie nodded. "You could say that."

Puffin shook his mane and trotted a little farther away.

"You've got to watch it when you're out with Puffin," Lizzie warned with a grin. "He has this habit of breaking into a gallop if you pass cantering ponies. I think it's his wild side showing through. You can tame New Forest ponies quite easily, but you might not ever completely take away that urge to run with the herd."

Quince's breath was warm on Mandy's hand as she stroked the pony's nose. "They're all gorgeous," she said honestly. "You're so lucky."

Lizzie beamed. "They are, aren't they?" she said in a rush. "And I do feel lucky. Every day."

The two girls grinned at each other. "Listen," said Lizzie. "I've got to clean out the field shelter." She pointed at a small wooden stable at one end of the field. "It won't take too long."

"I can help you, if you want," Mandy offered.

Lizzie stared at her. "Really?" she said, sounding surprised.

"Sure," Mandy nodded. "If we both do it, it'll be finished in half the time."

"Um, OK," said Lizzie uncertainly.

"Show me the shovel," Mandy declared, rolling up her sleeves and following Lizzie toward the shelter.

They worked side by side for half an hour. It was hot work, and Mandy soon forgot about her cold nose and chilled fingertips as she scattered clean, fresh-smelling straw around the stable. "There!" she declared with satisfaction, stepping back to admire her work. "All done — oh . . ."

She felt her foot skid in something slippery and she staggered, off balance.

"Watch out!" Lizzie called, but it was too late. As she frantically tried to stay upright, Mandy's feet shot in different directions and she landed flat on her bottom. Luckily, the fresh bed of straw cushioned her fall, but it didn't keep her from looking pretty funny on her way down.

Lizzie roared with laughter. "That was the funniest thing I've ever seen," she said, wiping her eyes with one hand and helping Mandy to her feet with the other. "You should do pantomime!"

Mandy grinned, wiping at a smear of muck on her legs. "Oh, boy, I'm going to stink."

"Don't worry," Lizzie reassured her. "I can lend you some clean clothes after we've ridden."

Mandy stared at her. "We're going riding?"

"I was going to ask if you'd like to ride with me today," Lizzie said, sounding a little nervous. "I mean, you obviously know your way around horses. Would you like to?"

Mandy was very touched. "Of course!" she exclaimed. "Thanks, Lizzie."

"There's a trail I know that will take us through the best part of the Forest," Lizzie said. "You can take Quince, and I'll ride Piper. Catch!"

She tossed a bridle toward Mandy, who grabbed it, unable to stop grinning from ear to ear. She had only been here a few hours, and she was already getting a chance to ride a New Forest pony!

The narrow path led them deep into the oldest part of the Forest. Mandy stared at the branches overhead, leaving Quince on a loose rein to pick her own way along the trail. She found that she noticed much more of her surroundings on horseback. She spotted a collection of sticks in a joint of a beech tree that looked like a squirrel's nest, and she noticed the way the deer had eaten the ivy growing on the tree trunks so that the trunks looked half brown and half green, where the deer couldn't reach the succulent leaves anymore. For once, she didn't mind that Lizzie wasn't very talkative. The only sound was the wind blowing through the branches and the gentle breathing of the ponies, plumes of mist spiraling up from their nostrils in the cold air.

When they trotted into a clearing beside a deep, silent stream, Mandy felt a rush of excitement. Standing in a cluster on the opposite side of the water stood a herd of ten or twelve wild ponies, munching quietly at the juicy, bright green grass. She checked to see whether Willow and Jingle were among them, but there was no sign of the gray mare and her little roan colt.

"How many ponies are there altogether in the Forest?" Mandy whispered.

"About three thousand, I think," Lizzie replied. "My dad would know. Counting the wild ponies is part of his job during the Drifts. That's when all the ponies are rounded up and checked. They do the Drifts from August to the end of October. It's a shame you missed them this year."

"Your dad checks *all* the ponies?" Mandy said in amazement. "How does he do that on his own?"

"He doesn't. He just does the ponies in this part of the Forest," Lizzie explained.

"But how can he tell if they're his ponies or not?" Mandy persisted. "I haven't seen any fences. What if the herds move around and get mixed in together?"

Lizzie pointed at a chestnut mare grazing with her hind-quarters toward them. "See that mare's tail?" she said.

Mandy saw that the chestnut's tail was cropped in a curious way — cut short on one side and left long on the other.

"That's how we can tell," Lizzie said. "Different districts in the New Forest have different ways of cutting the ponies' tails. There are brands, too, so my dad can tell who owns the individual ponies."

The chestnut swished her tail at them as Quince and Piper walked along the trail and away from the herd.

"What else happens during the Drifts, besides counting the ponies?" Mandy asked, breaking into a trot to keep up with Lizzie.

Lizzie ran through a list on her fingers. "Their teeth, their hooves, and their general health are all checked," she said. "It's really important for the ponies to be healthy as they approach winter. Sometimes they're sold, or the foals are taken to be weaned."

She glanced ahead to where the light was changing, growing brighter as the trees began to thin. "Come on!" she called, kicking Piper into a gallop. "Open ground ahead!"

Mandy closed her heels against Quince's sides and the little bay leaped forward. Laughing with delight, she urged Quince out of the trees and across the heath.

The wind tore through her hair, whipping it against her cheeks, and the only sound was Quince's hooves drumming on the peaty turf. This was the best feeling in the world!

"Look out for the bogs here," Lizzie called over her shoulder as they raced across the scrubby ground.

Mandy knew about bogs from the moors around Welford. You could always tell a bog from the plants that grew on and around it and the way the light threw a strange sheen on the watery soil. She spotted a suspicious-looking area to the left of the track and kept Quince well away from it, urging the little bay faster and faster until more woodland came into view on the far side of the heath.

"Phew!" Lizzie laughed, pulling Piper up before they reached the trees. She was breathing hard, her cheeks flushed and her eyes sparkling. "I needed that. You know that feeling sometimes, when you just want to run?"

Slowing Quince and nodding vigorously, Mandy shaded her eyes against the bright winter sun. Up ahead, two ponies were grazing to one side of the trees. "It's Willow and Jingle!" she realized. "Look, Lizzie — over there!"

"I thought they'd be somewhere nearby," Lizzie replied. "That was Willow's herd we passed by the stream back there. Whoa!"

There was a crashing sound deep in the woodland, and suddenly three brightly colored mountain bikes erupted from behind the trees. The boys on the bikes yelled loudly, pulling their front wheels up high to leap over tussocks of grass in a blur of red, blue, and yellow. Piper took one look at them and reared up in fright, scrabbling his front hooves in the air before tearing off into the trees. Quince shied and skittered to one side as the boys raced past, but Mandy managed to keep her under control.

"Lizzie!" Mandy yelled, watching as her friend galloped away, keeping her head low to avoid overhanging branches. "Hey!" She turned to shout angrily at the bikers, but the boys were long gone, mere pinpricks of color on the far side of the heath.

Then Mandy noticed Jingle. The colt was racing full speed across the rough grass, holding his tail high in fright. Willow was calling for him, shaking her mane and whinnying, but the colt wasn't listening. Clearly terrified, Jingle swerved and almost lost his footing on the track before veering away to the right — straight toward the bog.

With her heart in her mouth, Mandy turned Quince and kicked her toward the colt in the vain hope that she might be able to head him away from the bog.

"Jingle!" she called desperately. "Hey! Danger ahead! Danger!"

Jingle pushed himself on, his coat lathered in sweat. Mandy watched helplessly as he plunged knee-deep into the black, slimy murk — and almost immediately began to sink.

Four

Jingle whinnied in terror as his hooves disappeared beneath the surface of the bog. He reared and twisted, spraying mud through the air, and sank deeper the more he struggled. Willow neighed for her colt and galloped after him but remained a safe distance from the boggy ground, anxiously pacing on the dry, rough grass.

Mandy urged Quince across the heath as fast as the little bay could go. Not wanting to frighten Jingle any further, she slowed her pony down when she came closer to the bog and dismounted very slowly. She talked soothingly to the terrified colt as she looped

Quince's reins over a low-growing bush to one side of the boggy ground. Giving Quince a final pat, she edged toward the colt.

"Easy, Jingle," she murmured. The ground underfoot felt soft and watery, and Mandy stopped a couple of yards away from the struggling pony, not daring to move any closer yet.

Jingle's eyes were stretched wide, his ears flat against his head. Mandy could see that the bog wasn't deep enough for the young pony to drown, but it was deep enough for him to sprain a fetlock or break his leg if he didn't stop thrashing around. Willow whinnied again, and Jingle turned his head and looked toward the gray mare and Mandy.

Mandy knew she had to keep him calm. Thinking of all the scared animals she had dealt with in the past, she started to sing the first thing that came into her head. "Jingle bells, jingle bells, jingle all the way . . ." She reached out her hand, leaning across the boggy ground toward Jingle.

The frightened colt rolled his eyes toward her and kicked feebly, but at least he seemed to be listening. To Mandy's dismay, he sank a little deeper and was up to his belly now in the black, sticky mud. Reaching the end of "Jingle Bells," Mandy tried another song and inched closer to the colt. There was no sign of Lizzie, and she didn't dare leave Jingle to go for help. She'd have to try to pull him out herself.

"Here, boy, you're OK," she murmured, stretching her fingers until she could reach the tip of Jingle's soft, whiskery nose.

Jingle sighed and fixed her in his dark brown eyes as Mandy managed to twist her fingers through his mane. Then she began to pull, still singing every holiday carol she could think of. Very slowly, Jingle started to struggle toward her through the mud. Inch by inch, the young pony heaved himself out of the ooze, until he jerked his last back hoof free and stood on dry land.

Mandy's knees were trembling so much she thought she might fall over. Flinging her arms around Jingle's neck seemed the only way to stay upright. The semi-wild colt stood still, allowing Mandy to hug him as Willow nosed comfortingly at her foal, whickering from somewhere deep in her throat.

Someone was approaching, galloping hard across the heath. Jingle jerked his head up and stared over Mandy's shoulder.

"Are you OK?" Lizzie called, reining Piper in hard. "You're filthy! Did you end up in the bog?" She took in Jingle's muddy coat and brought her hand up to her

mouth in shock. "Jingle!" she said. "Did you rescue him from the bog? You did! You rescued him! Mandy, that's amazing!"

She scrambled down from Piper's back and looped his reins next to Quince's. "And you're *hugging* him!" she added in astonishment. "Do you realize how amazing that is? Jingle never lets people near him."

"Looks like that just changed," Mandy said shakily, scratching Jingle between the ears. "Are you all right? That was a heck of a gallop into the trees. I thought you were going to fall off."

Lizzie patted Piper, whose coat was dark with sweat. "We almost got to the other side of the forest before I could get him to stop," she said. "Those boys really scared him." Her brow darkened. "Grockles!" she exclaimed in disgust. "They can be so thoughtless sometimes."

Mandy gave Jingle a final scratch between the ears. "What are *grockles*?" she asked curiously.

Lizzie flushed. "It's what we call tourists," she said. "People who aren't from the Forest."

"Like me?" Mandy grinned. Jingle snuffled at her jacket and blew softly into her hand when she reached up to tickle his chin. Up close, his pinkish-gray coat was thistledown soft and flecked with white.

Lizzie's eyes sparkled. "Just like you," she said. "My dad will be so glad that Jingle's safe. Willow's foals have won lots of trophies in the past, and Jingle's showing signs of becoming a really good competition pony. The trainers and breeders who come to buy ponies at the Drifts will be very interested in him next autumn."

Willow whinnied and started to move back toward the trees. After a brief hesitation, Jingle gently pulled himself away from Mandy and trotted after his mother. The excitement of the past half hour suddenly passed, leaving Mandy feeling tired, dirty, and saddle sore. She picked up Quince's reins and pulled herself slowly into the saddle.

"You'll have to meet my dad," Lizzie said as they rode the ponies safely back to the Savages' field and dismounted by the field shelter. "Can you come over now?"

Mandy pulled off Quince's tack and brushed the dirt and mud off the leather as best she could. Then she looked down at herself. "Like this?" she joked, flicking at a spot of stinky bog mud on her knee. "I'm not sure your dad'll want to get too close."

"You don't have to stay long," Lizzie said earnestly, slinging Piper's bridle onto a hook in the tack room, which was next to the shelter.

"OK," said Mandy. "But I'll groom Quince first. Poor guy, I think he got more galloping than he bargained for today!"

She carefully brushed the little pony, then helped

Lizzie stuff some hay in the feed rack on the wall of the stable. Piper pushed greedily to the front and thrust his nose into the hay. Watching from the field, Puffin whinnied and came trotting over to join his friends.

Mandy gave Quince a final pat and pulled her hair behind her ears in an effort to look a little neater. "I guess I'm ready to see your dad, if you're sure he won't be too shocked."

Lizzie grinned. "I've got a feeling that my dad's going to like you," she said. "Even if you do smell like the bottom of a peat bog!"

"Look at you!" Dr. Emily exclaimed as Mandy trudged through the door of Beech End Cottage. "You need to get right into a warm bath before lunch!"

Mandy shrugged off her jacket and pulled off her muddy boots. "I've had a fantastic morning, Mom," she said as her mother shooed her through Great-Aunt Pip's kitchen and into the small pink bathroom at the back of the cottage.

"So I see," Dr. Emily said dryly, running the water so hard that the little bathroom was full of steam in seconds. "Made friends with every puddle in the New Forest, did you?"

Mandy slipped gratefully into the hot bath, letting the water soothe her aching muscles. "We had the most amazing ride," she said, "but then some cyclists made Piper bolt, and Jingle, this wild colt we saw, got stuck in a bog, so I rescued him."

Dr. Emily handed Mandy a washcloth so she could scrub the back of her neck. "I can always count on you to find trouble," she said. "Is the colt OK?"

Mandy nodded, dunking her hair back in the hot water. "Mr. Savage, Lizzie's dad, was really happy. Lizzie took me to meet him after we'd taken the ponies back to their field. Willow is a well-known brood mare, and apparently Jingle's really valuable. Plus he's the most adorable little colt I've ever known!" She paused, savoring the last piece of good news. "In fact, Mr. Savage was so glad I rescued Jingle that he's invited me along with him on his rounds tomorrow! Isn't that great?"

Her mom passed her a fluffy blue towel. "He was probably pleased that Lizzie had made a friend as well," she said. "What do you think you'll be doing tomorrow?"

"Checking on the ponies," Mandy said, twisting the towel in her ears to get every last drop of moisture out. "Talking to the commoners — they're the Forest people who own the ponies — about their fencing and their ponies' health. Lots of things."

"You sound like an Agister already!" Dr. Emily said, and laughed.

"Lizzie says that a day out with her dad will tell me more about the New Forest than a week doing the tourist trails," Mandy told her mother.

Ten minutes later, dressed in warm gym pants and an old wool cardigan, Mandy sat at Great-Aunt Pip's kitchen table. Her dad was standing at the stove with a kitchen towel slung over his shoulder and a wooden spoon in his hand.

"The first Noel, the angels did say," he sang, waving the spoon in time to the music on the radio, "was to certain poor shepherds in fields where they lay. . . ."

"Look out, Dad!" Mandy protested as a blob of pasta sauce flew off the end of the spoon and landed on the table.

"That's a nice voice you have there, Adam," Great-Aunt Pip observed as she carried a pot of pasta to the table. "We could use you in the choir for the Christmas service. In fact, I'm recruiting you here and now. Rehearsal tonight in the church, OK?"

It wasn't easy to say no to Great-Aunt Pip, as Mandy had already discovered. She grinned at her mom, who rolled her eyes.

"Thank you, Pip," said Dr. Adam, placing the pasta sauce on the table with a flourish. "I'd love to."

Great-Aunt Pip looked at Mandy's mom and opened

her mouth. Dr. Emily raised a hand. "Before you ask, Pip, you should know that my voice cracks glass," she said.

Great-Aunt Pip frowned. "It's not really that bad, is it? We could always use more voices at Christmas."

Dr. Emily lifted her shoulders apologetically. "I'd give you a demonstration, but I might curdle the sauce," she said.

Great-Aunt Pip looked disappointed. "Oh, well," she said, ladling out helpings of steaming pasta and creamy sauce and passing it around the table. "I'm sure we'll find a use for you somewhere in the holiday proceedings."

"My mom makes a mean mince pie," Mandy put in.

"Perfect!" Great-Aunt Pip exclaimed. "We always have refreshments after our last choir practice. Tim Savage usually makes the mince tarts, but I'm sure he'd appreciate a little help this year."

"Speaking of Mr. Savage," said Dr. Emily, looking at Mandy, "one of us has some great news."

Full of excitement again, Mandy told everyone about her adventure that morning and her plans for the following day.

Great-Aunt Pip nodded with approval. "You've obviously made an excellent impression, Mandy," she said. "Good for you. Now, anyone for coffee? We can sit by the fire in the living room."

Mandy offered to do the dishes. Then she brought a tray of coffee and homemade spice cookies into the little living room, which was scented by the pine candles burning merrily on the mantelpiece. Mandy set the tray down on the coffee table beside the fire and settled down in an armchair. Feeling pleasantly sleepy, she looked around for Pyramus, hoping to coax him onto her lap.

The gray cat was sitting beside the baseboard beneath the window, his paws tucked underneath him. Mandy clicked her tongue hopefully at him, but the cat ignored her. "Pyramus?" she said, reaching her fingers toward him. "Is everything OK, boy?"

"Don't worry about him," said Great-Aunt Pip, stirring sugar into a cup of coffee and handing it to Mandy's dad. "I think there's a mouse behind that baseboard. He tends to ignore everything else when there's a chance of some hunting."

Mandy clicked her tongue again, but Pyramus merely shifted his weight and stayed crouched where he was. Giving up, she helped herself to a cookie. It was still warm, and the taste of cinnamon and raisins was heavenly. With a contented sigh, she settled back in the armchair and closed her eyes. She could hardly believe she'd only been in the New Forest for twenty-four hours. So much had happened — meeting Lizzie, then meeting

Willow and Jingle, riding Quince, the whole drama
with the bog, and now the promise of a ride with Mr.
Savage the following day. It wasn't long before she
slipped into a light doze, dreaming about Jingle in the
show ring, his mane decked with ribbons and Mandy on
his back waving proudly at the cheering crowds.

Five

Early the next morning, Mandy walked through the woodland toward the Savages' field, where she had arranged to meet Lizzie and her father. She felt more confident about finding the path through the trees than she had the previous day. The Forest was especially beautiful in the pale daylight, and the low-lying mist made the ground look like a silvery lake.

It wasn't long before she reached the pasture on the other side of the road. Lizzie and her dad were standing beside the shelter saddling the ponies. The ground around the entrance was more churned up than ever.

Lizzie looked up from tightening Piper's girth and waved as Mandy crunched over the frosty mud toward them.

"You're good and early!" Tim Savage smiled at Mandy. He had the same wide-spaced eyes and freckled nose as his daughter. Mandy decided that if Lizzie was like a porcupine, Mr. Savage was more like a stag, with his broad shoulders and dark eyes. To her disappointment, he wasn't wearing his Agister uniform, but was dressed in dark jeans and a padded jacket.

"We only wear the uniform on special occasions," Mr. Savage explained when Mandy asked him about it. "It's not very practical for everyday."

Lizzie adjusted Puffin's stirrups and beckoned Mandy over. "You're on this guy today," she said, giving Mandy a leg up.

Puffin chewed noisily on his bit as Mandy adjusted the strap on her helmet and gathered up the reins.

"Watch out for that little galloping habit of his," Mr. Savage said with a wink. "He almost took me all the way to Lymington a couple of weeks ago when we passed a group of wild ponies going the other way."

"He's kidding," Lizzie whispered as they trotted out of the field and onto the road. "Puff's fine most of the time. You have nothing to worry about."

Mandy reached down to pat Puffin's shaggy gray neck.

"If he runs off, I'll make sure I remember the way back!" she said, sounding more optimistic than she felt.

They walked slowly through the forest, keeping the ponies in single file along the rutted track that led to the town of Woodhurst. Mr. Savage wanted to make a few phone calls from his office before they set out on their rounds. The Agister's long legs looked funny astride the small, stocky pony, but Quince carried Mr. Savage as easily as if he were a feather. Mandy closed her eyes for a moment and breathed in the woody smell of the trees. To her relief, Puffin walked steadily along the track behind the others, showing no signs of bolting off the path.

When they reached the town, Mr. Savage dismounted beside a neat wooden hut and tied Quince's reins to one of several tethering posts on the side of the road. Mandy decided they were a New Forest version of a bike rack and grinned to herself. Imagine riding to work every day on a pony!

"I won't be long," Mr. Savage said, unlocking the office door. "Did you eat breakfast before you left, Mandy?"

She shook her head. "There wasn't time."

"We had the same problem," Mr. Savage said. "But we have a long day ahead, and we need some food inside us. Lizzie, could you take Mandy and get us all something to eat?"

"There's a good place on the main street," said Lizzie. "Dad likes the coffee there. Come on, Mandy."

They left the ponies tied to the posts and walked along the road. Woodhurst was very quiet and slightly eerie in the morning mist. There was a church, a cluster of small brick cottages, a couple of gift shops, and a café with brightly lit windows and the appetizing smell of warm bread and fresh coffee wafting out of the door. Mandy followed Lizzie as she pushed open the door and called a cheerful greeting to the middle-aged woman behind the counter.

"Coffee as usual, Lizzie?" said the woman with a smile.

"Thanks, Mrs. Graves," Lizzie said, stamping her feet and blowing on her hands. "Plus two hot chocolates for us, and can we take three of your waffles, too? This is my friend Mandy, by the way. She's visiting the Forest for a few days."

"Out with the Agister, are you, dear?" Mrs. Graves asked Mandy as she placed three waffles into a paper bag. "There's no better way to see the real Forest."

"That's what everyone keeps telling me." Mandy smiled, reaching over to take the bag.

Mrs. Graves filled a paper cup with steaming black coffee and put on a lid. "Strong, just the way your dad likes it," she said, passing the cup to Lizzie. "Careful where you ride today. I nearly fell on a patch of ice by the church this morning. Gave me the scare of my life!"

"It's nice that everyone's so friendly here," Mandy said as they walked back toward the Agister's office. "It reminds me of Welford, where I live. Sometimes I feel as if I have the biggest family in the world!"

"I've known Mrs. Graves all my life," Lizzie agreed. "That's the way the Forest works, too."

Mr. Savage glanced up from the phone as Lizzie and Mandy came in. He mouthed his thanks before turning back to the phone. Mandy flopped down in a worn old armchair by the gas fire to munch on her waffle. It was buttery and delicious, packed with juicy raisins.

"We'll be over as soon as we can," Mr. Savage was saying, jotting something down on a pad by his computer. "If it's as bad as it sounds, we may need to call in the vet."

Mandy sat up.

"There's a pony caught on some barbed wire a little way north of here," Mr. Savage told them, putting down the phone. "We'd better check it out right away. I hope it's not too serious. Steve — that's our local vet — is away for the holidays. We could call in the backup, but he's over on the other side of the Forest."

"My mom or dad would help," Mandy suggested, following Mr. Savage and Lizzie outside. "I'm sure they won't mind."

"I'll remember that," Mr. Savage promised. "But perhaps it's something we can deal with on our own." He locked up the office and untied the ponies. "It's only a ten-minute ride from here," he explained, vaulting onto Quince's back.

Mandy was surprised. "Aren't we going back to get the Land Rover?"

Mr. Savage shook his head. "It would take three times longer," he said. "With the ponies, we don't have to stick to the roads. We can cut through the Forest instead."

They trotted down the street, the ponies' shoes ringing out on the cold pavement. Mandy dug her heels into Puffin's sides to keep up with the others. On the far side of the town, Mr. Savage turned Quince off the road and through a gate onto a wide gravel path. He urged the little bay into a canter, and Mandy and Lizzie followed.

Five minutes later, Mandy could see that Lizzie hadn't been exaggerating about the strength of the New Forest ponies. Quince showed no signs of tiring despite her heavy load. Puffin was cantering effortlessly beside Piper with his neck stretched out, his breath sounding deep and even as they flew along the path.

Suddenly, Mandy heard galloping hooves ahead. She

looked up, expecting to see another group of riders. Instead, three or four wild ponies raced across the path ahead of them and disappeared into the trees. Puffin snorted and snatched at the reins, trying to swerve after them.

"Whoa!" Mandy hauled on the reins until she felt as if her arms were about to come out of their sockets. With a grumpy toss of his head, Puffin skidded to a halt at the edge of the path, looking longingly after the disappearing ponies.

"Come on, boy," Mandy coaxed him. "If you want to run with the herd, try sticking with Piper and Quince, please!"

Giving a final snort, Puffin meekly turned back onto the pathway, and Mandy sent him thundering after the others who were now ahead.

At the far end of the track was a stretch of heathland where a barbed-wire fence separated the open land from a grove of fir trees. A stocky red-faced man was waiting anxiously by the fence.

"Morning, Andrew," Mr. Savage greeted him. "Where's this pony?"

"I got him out of the wire as best I could," the man said. "But there's a nasty tear on his shoulder. I think he'll need stitching up."

"Remember Mrs. Graves at the café?" Lizzie whispered to Mandy as they followed Andrew around the corner to where a pony was tethered to a bush. "This is her husband."

The pony was taller than any other New Forest ponies Mandy had seen since her arrival. Broad and strong-looking, he flinched as Mr. Savage gently examined the cut on his neck. "It's deep, all right," he told Mr. Graves. "Let's get him back to your place, Andrew. We'll get a vet over to you." He looked apologetically at Mandy. "Looks like we'll be needing your parents after all. Some vacation, eh?"

"They won't mind," Mandy assured him. "Dad always has his vet bag with him."

Mr. Savage pulled out a cell phone and punched in Great-Aunt Pip's number. It was funny seeing a piece of modern technology after their strange, old-fashioned morning. For all the New Forest's wonderful traditions, the modern world had its advantages.

Dr. Adam answered the phone immediately and promised to get there as soon as he could. Mr. Graves's house was just over the ridge. Moving slowly so the injured pony wouldn't lose too much blood, they walked into the trees where a small, neat bungalow stood. *It doesn't look like the kind of place where people keep horses*, Mandy thought with surprise. But around the back of the house was a small yard with three nice stalls. Mr. Graves led the pony carefully into the closest one.

"What's his name?" Mandy asked, dismounting from Puffin and leaning over the door to scratch the pony gently between the ears.

"Scallywag," Mr. Graves told her. "He's a bit of a troublemaker in the Forest. I always get calls about him knocking down fences or eating young trees."

Mandy tickled Scallywag under the chin, and the pony responded by pressing his head against her shoulder. Right now, he was obviously feeling much too sorry for himself to get into any mischief.

Adam Hope arrived ten minutes later in the car. Mr. Savage introduced him to Andrew Graves, and the two men shook hands.

"You poor old boy," Dr. Adam murmured, stroking the pony's neck. "Scallywag, is it? Well, Scallywag, we'll fix you up in no time. Mandy, can you give me a hand?" He opened his bag and passed her a pair of surgical gloves. "Perhaps Lizzie can hold his head while we stitch this fellow up."

Lizzie looked impressed. "Do you help your dad much at the clinic?" she asked.

"Yes. Just like you help yours in the Forest," Mandy pointed out, handing her dad some antiseptic swabs.

Lizzie soothed the worried pony, who kept trying to

turn its head and bite Dr. Adam. "I wouldn't be able to do that," she admitted. "I'd be too afraid of hurting the ponies."

Mandy shrugged. "Sometimes you just have to have faith that whatever you're doing will make them feel better in the long run." She glanced at Lizzie. "But it's tricky sometimes, especially when the animal is in a lot of pain."

"That should do it," Dr. Adam told Andrew Graves, finishing a neat row of stitches and giving Scallywag an encouraging pat. "Keep him out of the Forest for a few days, just in case he opens up the wound again."

"Thanks so much, Adam," said Mr. Savage. "I really appreciate you taking time out of your vacation for this."

"A vet's never really on vacation," Dr. Adam said, and smiled. "Isn't that right, Mandy?"

After dealing with Mr. Graves's pony, Mandy's dad drove back to Woodhurst while they visited a small farm deep in the Forest, where Mr. Savage tagged the ears of some cattle. Then they headed back to the office. Mandy was beginning to realize that Agisters spent a lot of their time doing routine administration work as well as performing heroic animal rescues — just like vets!

"OK," Mr. Savage declared at twelve-thirty, putting

down the phone. "I think it's time for lunch, don't you? I could eat a horse."

"I don't think that's part of an Agister's job description, Dad," Lizzie teased. "We'll go get some sandwiches from the café."

The town was much busier than it had been at seven-thirty that morning. Cars were parked along the road, colored lights twinkled around the front porches, and the gift shops looked as if they were having great holiday sales. Mandy glanced hopefully at the sky, but there was no sign of snow. *There's still a couple of days until Christmas,* she told herself, imagining how beautiful the Forest would look all white and silent on Christmas Day.

As they approached the café, Mandy came out of her daydream with a thump. She tugged Lizzie's arm. "Do you see those boys?" she whispered, pointing at a group of three boys at a small table outside the café. A row of mountain bikes was propped against the wall beside them. "I think they're the ones who frightened Jingle yesterday!"

Lizzie frowned. "You're right," she said. "I'm going to talk to them."

Mandy watched in astonishment as Lizzie marched fearlessly across the street and came to a stop beside the table where the boys were sitting. "Were you riding on the heath yesterday?" she demanded.

The boys looked surprised. "Yeah," said one of them. "So what?"

"I just thought you should know that you frightened two ponies so badly that one bolted and the other nearly broke his leg in a bog," Lizzie said.

The boys looked shocked. "Are they OK?" asked the tallest one.

"Yes," Lizzie said. "No thanks to you."

There was an embarrassed silence.

"Can you please remember to ride more carefully in the future?" Lizzie said.

"Sure."

"Yeah."

"Will do." The boys mumbled their replies, sounding as if they genuinely meant it while they stared down at the table.

"Thanks." Lizzie turned and walked back to Mandy.

"You really told them!" Mandy exclaimed, looking back at the subdued group of boys.

"Good," Lizzie said simply.

They spent a busy afternoon riding around the Forest trails, and checking the condition of the ponies. When they found a pony that was lame or overly thin, Mandy and Lizzie helped to find the pony's brand in its shaggy winter coat and Mr. Savage made a phone call to the owners, asking them to take their pony back to their stables until it was well enough to return to the Forest.

"It's getting dark," Mandy said with surprise as she glanced around her. "I had no idea it was so late."

"Time flies when you're out here," said Mr. Savage. "In the summer I'm frequently out until nine-thirty at night, because it's still light and I don't realize what time it is."

Up ahead there was a large wooden lodge set back from the road, the kind Mandy associated with skiing vacations and mountains.

"That's Mom's gallery," Lizzie said. "Do you mind if we go in? I need to pick up a gift I asked her to put aside for me."

"Sure," Mr. Savage nodded. "You've been a great help today. Don't forget to bring the ponies back to the house tonight, Lizzie. We're keeping them at home for a few weeks until their field dries out."

Mandy remembered the empty field outside her window. "So, I'll be able to see the ponies out my window every morning for the rest of my stay?" she said hopefully.

"Looks like it." Lizzie smiled at her.

Mandy had always thought having a clinic full of animals attached to the house was the best thing in the world. Now she wasn't so sure. Imagine waking up every day to see your own ponies from your bedroom window!

Inside, Mrs. Savage's gallery smelled of warm polished wood. Mandy looked around at the paintings hung on the walls and the sculptures and pottery lining the windowsills. Then her eye fell on a wooden sculpture sitting on a base beside the door.

It was a fox, but Mandy wasn't sure how she knew

that. The wood was barely carved at all, but somehow the sculptor had given it a foxy spirit, with a long, thick tail and the gliding motion of a hunting vixen. She walked over and glanced at the price tag wistfully. It was much more than she could afford, especially as she still had a couple of Christmas gifts to buy.

"What do you think of it?"

Mandy looked up to see a woman with short blond hair smiling at her. "I think it's wonderful," she said honestly.

The woman looked pleased. "It's one of mine," she said. "I'm Helen, Lizzie's mom. You must be Mandy. Lizzie's been telling me all about you. Lizzie, don't forget we have a rehearsal tonight."

"What rehearsal?" Mandy said.

"We sing in the local church choir," Mrs. Savage explained. "We're rehearsing for the Christmas service at the moment."

"That must be the same choir Great-Aunt Pip's asked Dad to sing in!" Mandy realized. "Does your dad sing as well?"

"Oh, no, Dad's got a terrible voice," Lizzie said cheerfully. "But he makes great mince tarts for our last rehearsal."

"Great-Aunt Pip mentioned that," Mandy recalled. "I

think she might have volunteered me and Mom to help your dad with the refreshments this year."

Mrs. Savage laughed. "That sounds like Pip," she said. "She organizes everything around here."

With one last, longing glance at the fox sculpture, Mandy followed Lizzie outside to retrieve the ponies. Unlooping Puffin's reins from the tethering post, Mandy glanced up at the dark sky. When would it *snow*? All those festive gifts, the Christmas music that had been softly playing on the gallery's stereo, and the twinkling lights in the windows were starting to make her feel really Christmassy.

Snow will make everything perfect, she thought. But maybe it was too much to hope for. . . .

Six

"Hey, lazybones!" Dr. Emily's voice drifted up the stairs. "Time to get up!"

Mandy snuggled deeper under the quilt. After helping Lizzie to stable the ponies the day before, she'd helped her mom and Great-Aunt Pip with some chores and had a long hot bath before supper. By the time she finished her dessert, Mandy had been so tired that she could barely put on her pajamas and get into bed.

Mandy turned over and caught sight of the clock beside her bed. Nine-thirty! She couldn't remember the last time she'd slept so late. She dragged on her clothes, ran a brush quickly through her hair, and made her way downstairs.

Pyramus was sitting on his usual step in the pine-scented hall. Just in time, Mandy remembered to step over him. "You're going to be stepped on someday, Pyramus," she warned, crouching down to tickle the gray cat under the chin.

Pyramus gave a strange, wheezing cough and hunched his shoulders. Frowning, Mandy looked more closely at him. His eyes were half shut, and his coat looked strangely dull. She carefully felt along the cat's body, checking for any injuries. He seemed much bonier than she remembered.

"Mom!" she called. "I think there's something wrong with Pyramus."

Dr. Emily put her head around the kitchen door. "Bring him into the kitchen," she suggested. "I'll take a look at him."

Mandy scooped up the cat and carried him carefully along the hall. He felt light in her arms as she set him down in her mother's arms. He didn't move when Dr. Emily petted him, except to give a plaintive meow.

Great-Aunt Pip put her coffee down, looking anxious. "He doesn't seem right at all," she said. "I didn't see him all day yesterday, now that I think about it. Do you know what's the matter with him, Emily?"

Dr. Emily reached down with one hand and opened the vet bag that was just beside the back door. She listened to Pyramus's heartbeat and then put the stetho-scope against his chest. Finally, she took his temperature. "His breathing is very shallow and his temperature is up," she said, shaking the thermometer to reset the reading. "Is he vaccinated against cat flu, Pip?"

Great-Aunt Pip nodded. "Oh, yes."

"Well, that's good," Dr. Emily said. "Whatever it is, he's having difficulty breathing. I think we should keep him inside for a couple of days. It's important that his chest doesn't get chilled in this bitter weather. Do you have a litter box?"

"I still have the one we used when he was a kitten." Great-Aunt Pip leaned over to stroke Pyramus comfort-ingly.

"Where's Dad?" Mandy asked. "We should ask him what he thinks."

"Ask what I think about what?" Dr. Adam came in with a blast of cold air and hung his coat and scarf on the peg by the back door.

Mandy explained that Pyramus wasn't well. Like her mom had done, Dr. Adam listened to Pyramus's chest.

"It sounds like pneumonia, but I can't say for sure," he said, straightening up.

"That would fit the symptoms," Dr. Emily agreed.

Mandy got a cushion from the living room and set it down beside the fireplace. They settled Pyramus down with a bowl of water. Pyramus tried to purr but started coughing instead.

"Poor old thing," Great-Aunt Pip said. "Will he be OK?"

"You're lucky to have a couple of vets as houseguests, Pip," Dr. Adam said, giving her an encouraging smile. "He's a young cat so he should recover easily enough with a little extra care. We'll keep an eye on him for a couple of days, and if he shows no signs of improving we could try antibiotics."

"Where have you been, anyway, Dad?" Mandy said.

"Tim called me out again," Dr. Adam said, pouring a cup of coffee. "There was a lame pony in the Forest. Its hoof was infected from stepping on a rusty soda can that someone had thrown into some undergrowth. It astonishes me how thoughtless people can be sometimes."

He took a long swallow of coffee and sighed with pleasure. "Ah, that's better," he said. "My voice feels as raw as that poor old pony's foot. I'm not used to all this singing."

"Was the choir rehearsal last night fun?" Mandy asked, sitting on the floor by the stove so she could pet Pyramus. She'd gone to bed before her dad got back.

Dr. Adam grinned. "It was great," he said. "Except for me. I managed to sing really loudly in a silent part and felt pretty silly. Hope I don't do that in the Christmas service."

"That's what rehearsals are for," Mandy said comfortingly. "So you can make mistakes in private."

"There was nothing private about this!" Dr. Adam laughed. "I thought the echo would never die! I should be better at tonight's rehearsal."

"That reminds me," Great-Aunt Pip said. "We're all going over there to help Tim with the refreshments later, aren't we? I have a great recipe for hot spiced orange juice — it's wonderful for tired voices. I'll give the Savages a call and find out when would be a good time to get there."

Mandy munched on toast and jam and stared out the window. The sky was such a bright blue that it hurt to look at it. Frost lay in patches around the bottom of the trees where the sunlight hadn't touched the ground. "Is it OK if I go out for a while?" she asked her parents.

"Seeing Lizzie again?" her mom guessed.

Mandy shook her head. "I want to see if I can find Jingle."

"Just stay warm," her mom warned. "I don't want you coming down with pneumonia as well."

There was no sign of Jingle anywhere. Mandy stayed out in the icy air for as long as she could, retracing her steps and looking hard in every nook and shadow of the great oak trees. She tried whistling a few bars of "Jingle Bells" in case Jingle recognized it, but it was no good. The colt and his mother were nowhere to be seen.

"It's like they've vanished into thin air," she said gloomily as her mother handed her a plate of lasagna at lunchtime. "They're *ponies*, not squirrels. How can something so big hide so well?"

"They aren't wild ponies for nothing," her dad said. "They know the Forest far better than you, Mandy. Jingle and his mother don't want to be found today, that's all."

Mandy sighed and toyed with her food. She'd looked for Jingle yesterday, too, but even though they'd ridden across what felt like half the Forest, they hadn't seen him. She and her parents were only staying at Beech End Cottage for a few more days. She'd felt a real connection with the young horse when she'd rescued him from the bog. It seemed a shame that she wasn't going to get a chance to build it into a real relationship.

Mandy dried the dishes after lunch and then helped Great-Aunt Pip to light the fire in the living room for Pyramus. The cat wasn't looking much better and coughed mournfully as Mandy placed him on a cushion next to the fireplace.

"Is there anything else we can do for him?" Great-Aunt Pip asked, petting her cat. "I hate to see him suffering like this."

"Try to be patient," Dr. Adam advised. "We'll just keep him quiet for a few days. I'm sure he'll improve soon."

"I'll go down to Woodhurst this afternoon and see if I can get him some kitty treats," Great-Aunt Pip said. "Then we can all go over to the Savages'. Mince tarts don't make themselves, I've been told!"

Mandy knew she was trying to stay cheerful for her visitors' benefit, but she could tell by the way Great-Aunt Pip kept glancing back at Pyramus that she was really worried about her cat. Mandy traced her finger around the outline of Pyramus's ear and hoped for the hundredth time that there was nothing seriously wrong with him. He looked so frail and listless that it was getting harder and harder to believe he would get better by himself.

Mandy's mom went to the village with Great-Aunt Pip to buy the cat treats. When they returned, Pyramus ignored the tidbits, closing his eyes and tucking his nose between his paws as if he couldn't bear the smell of them. He didn't look good.

"There's nothing more we can do until we're know exactly what we're dealing with," Dr. Adam said, patting

Great-Aunt Pip on the shoulder. "He's in the best place for now, I promise."

Great-Aunt Pip tickled the gray cat between the ears, but Pyramus didn't look up. "Well," she said briskly after a moment. "We'd better get our things together for the baking session. Emily and I bought some ingredients when we were in the village — orange juice, honey, lemons, cinnamon sticks, and cloves. I'll bring along a few thermoses, to keep it all hot. Tim will have everything we need for the mince tarts."

"Except my secret ingredient," Dr. Emily said, smiling and fishing in her bag. "Ground almonds," she said with satisfaction, producing a small packet. "It does wonders for the pastry dough."

"Are you coming, Dad?" Mandy asked, reaching for her scarf.

Dr. Adam cleared his throat. "I've, er, got a rehearsal today, remember?"

"That's not until four o'clock," Mandy said, frowning.

"Yes, well, I've got to do a couple of other things to do this afternoon," her dad replied without looking at her. He pulled on his coat and slipped out the door. "See you later."

"What was that about, Mom?" Mandy asked, feeling puzzled.

Dr. Emily shrugged. "You know how mysterious your

dad can be sometimes," she said lightly. "Come on. We'd better head over to Clearfield Cottage."

Even though it only took two minutes to walk to the Savages' house, everyone wrapped up warmly. The temperature had dropped even more, and the tip of Mandy's nose started tingling as soon as they stepped out the door. The sharp blue of the morning had been replaced by gloomy, yellowish-looking clouds.

"You said it doesn't snow much in the New Forest, didn't you, Great-Aunt Pip?" Mandy said as they crunched through the frosty yard.

"It's very rare," Great-Aunt Pip replied.

Mandy grinned. "Well, I think it's going to snow soon," she announced. "We get clouds just like that in Yorkshire most winters, and then it almost always snows."

Great-Aunt Pip looked pleased. "How wonderful!" she said. "The Forest in the snow is a beautiful sight, but it's only happened twice in all the years I've lived here. I really hope you're right, Mandy. It would put the finishing touch on Christmas."

They turned up the Savages' driveway. Mandy looked around when she heard a whinny and was pleased to see Quince trotting across the pasture to say hello.

"I'll just be a minute," she called to the others, who waved and walked toward the house. "Hey, there, girl," she said, running one gloved hand up Quince's brown ears and stroking her nose with the other. "How's your new field?"

Quince snickered quietly and blew warm, steaming air out of her nostrils. Mandy thought wistfully about Jingle, hoping he'd find somewhere warm for shelter if it did snow.

When she turned to follow the others, she saw an odd shape lying under a tarpaulin beside the gate. Whatever was hidden was square-looking and stood high off the ground, with what looked like two poles jutting out at one end. Mandy thought about it for a moment, then gave Quince one last pat before heading toward the warm lights of the house.

Mr. Savage opened the front door with a smile and a smudge of flour on the end of his nose. "Welcome to the mince tart factory," he said, taking Mandy's coat. "Come on in. It's all hands on deck this afternoon."

The kitchen was full of steam and the scent of orange peel and mincemeat. Judging from the pile of dishes in the drying rack, it looked as if Mr. Savage had used every single pan in the house so far.

"Where's Lizzie?" Mandy asked, rolling up her sleeves and putting on the striped apron that Mr. Savage handed to her.

"She groomed Piper when she brought him in and transferred all the mud from him to her!" Mr. Savage said. "So she's up having a bath."

Mandy frowned. "If Piper's already in his stable, why's Quince still in the field?"

Mr. Savage's eyes twinkled. "That's for me to know and you to find out," he teased. "Now, let's get down to business. We've got four hours to make seventy mince tarts, bake them, put them into baskets, and take them over to the church. Let's get moving!"

Dr. Emily added her ground almonds to the pastry, and Mandy rolled it and cut it out. Then she pressed the pastry into the tart pans and helped Mr. Savage to fill each one with mincemeat. Lizzie came downstairs in time to help cut out small circles and stars of pastry to place decoratively on the top of each tart. Mandy was kept so busy that she barely had time to wave at Lizzie when she left for rehearsal at three-thirty.

Because the Savages' stove was small, they had to bake the tarts in three batches, so it was more than two hours before the last batch of piping hot tarts was pulled gently from the oven. Mandy couldn't resist trying one as she put them onto wire racks to cool. It was just as good as Lizzie had promised.

Mr. Savage produced three baskets lined with red-and-green fabric and decorated with ivy twisted around the handles. "We just need to fill these and we're ready to go," he instructed. "How's the orange juice coming along, Pip?"

Great-Aunt Pip lifted a pan off the stove and poured the steaming, scented orange juice carefully into three thermoses. "Just about finished," she said with satisfaction, tightening the lids and putting the thermoses alongside the mince tarts in the baskets.

Mr. Savage stood back to admire their feast. "That has to be the best-looking bunch of mince tarts the Woodhurst choir will ever see," he declared. "Now, I think we all deserve a treat. Give me ten minutes, then get your coats on, bring a basket each, and come outside."

Mandy watched him leave the kitchen and wondered exactly what he was up to. She hopped from one foot to the other as she waited for at least nine of the minutes he had asked for, then pulled on her coat and burst out the front door.

She gasped. The tarpaulin had been pulled off the strange square object to reveal a polished wooden one-horse carriage, just big enough for four people. It was standing on the driveway in front of Clearfield Cottage with two pretty lanterns hanging on either side of the driver's seat. Bells were attached to the lanterns, and big white cushions and a pile of warm checked blankets lined the backseat. Quince stood patiently harnessed between the shafts, her breath rising in steamy clouds.

"It's beautiful!" Mandy cried.

"Lizzie and I decorated it earlier. After all that hard work, we may as well travel to the rehearsal in style." Mr. Savage smiled and produced something from behind his back. "All we need is the finishing touch." He carefully fixed a set of sparkling felt-covered antlers to Quince's bridle. "It's time for a Christmas ride you'll never forget!"

Seven

"Is this another New Forest tradition?" Mandy asked, going over to stroke Quince's nose.

Mr. Savage shook his head. "Nope, just an old Savage one! Here, let me give you a leg up."

He helped Mandy, her mom, and her great-aunt into the carriage and tucked the blankets around their legs. Hopping into the driver's seat, he clicked his tongue and shook the reins. Quince walked forward and the trap moved off with a tiny jerk. The wheels made a faint rumbling sound and the bells tinkled merrily as they rolled down to the road that led through the Forest.

"This really is traveling in style! I wonder if I should

tell Adam to trade in the Land Rover," Dr. Emily joked, pulling the blanket closer around her knees.

As Quince broke into a trot and sent the wheels of the carriage spinning lightly along behind her, Mandy gazed around at the Forest. There was a bright moon tonight, and the trees threw surprisingly sharp black shadows across their path.

"A badger!" Great-Aunt Pip exclaimed, leaning forward and staring into the trees.

Mandy twisted in her seat. "Where?"

"His striped face is very effective camouflage in the moonlight," Dr. Emily said. "He's by the base of that beech tree."

Mandy stared hard at the dappled, moonlit ground. After a moment, the black-and-white shadows moved, and Mandy saw a sharp face and two rounded black ears. The badger was sniffing around the base of the tree, unperturbed by the sight of the nighttime visitors.

The road passed out of the trees and across some heathland. The moonlight seemed even brighter out here, and Mandy could make out individual blades of grass. Up ahead, a pool of water glimmered, and around the pool were the silhouettes of three ponies.

Mandy sat up and peered closer. Two of the silhouettes looked familiar. One was wide and sturdy-looking, and beside it was the unmistakable outline of a young colt whose tail hadn't yet grown to its full length.

"It's Willow and Jingle!" she cried, grabbing her mother's arm. "I'm sure of it!" Happiness surged through her. As if the evening hadn't been perfect enough already!

"If it is, I'd like to take a look at Jingle," said Mr. Savage. "Just to make sure he's OK after his bog adventure."

He reined Quince to a standstill. The three ponies looked up from the pool and stared at the carriage. Jingle let out a shrill whinny.

"He knows it's me!" Mandy said, almost bursting with delight as she climbed down from her seat. Holding out her hand, she moved slowly toward him. "Hey, there, boy. I haven't seen you for a few days."

Jingle whinnied again and pushed his nose into Mandy's outstretched hand. Willow snorted jealously.

Mr. Savage gave a low whistle. "That's amazing," he said. "Lizzie was right. You're a real hit with him. He's usually very cautious around people."

Mandy brought her hand up to stroke Jingle's mane. "He looks OK, doesn't he, Mr. Savage?" she asked anxiously. "I've been worried about him."

Mr. Savage held out his hand to the colt. Wary, Jingle pressed closer to Mandy, but he allowed Mr. Savage to stroke his nose and run his hand down his withers. The Agister knelt down and examined Jingle's legs with a practiced hand.

"He looks fine," he said at last, straightening up with a smile.

"He looks more than just fine," Great-Aunt Pip said, sounding excited as she leaned out of the carriage. "He's the *image* of a pony I used to ride many years ago, Highfields Faraway."

The air was suddenly charged with an excitement that Mandy didn't understand. "Who was Highfields Faraway?" she asked.

"He was one of the best show ponies the New Forest has ever produced," Mr. Savage said. He stared thoughtfully at Jingle. "I never knew him, but he's legendary in the Forest. And if I'm right, Pip, he won more ribbons than any Forest pony before or since."

Great-Aunt Pip nodded. "With a coat that color and that shape of head, Jingle must be related," she said with absolute certainty in her voice. "Tim, I understand you have plans to show Jingle in the ring. Well, let me tell you this. If Jingle is related to Highfields Faraway, you could have a future *star* of the show ring on your hands."

Mandy leaned her face against Jingle's whiskery cheek. "I knew you were special," she whispered to the colt, who snuffled softly into her hair.

Mr. Savage checked his watch. "We'd better get moving or the choir won't get their tarts," he said. "Mandy, would you like to drive the carriage the rest of the way?"

"Are you sure?" she asked, surprised and flattered.

"I'll take the risk." Mr. Savage grinned.

Mandy took up Quince's reins very carefully. Following Mr. Savage's instructions, she clicked her tongue and shook the reins. Quince immediately started to walk. There was a slight jerk as her harness strained against the shafts, and then the carriage rolled forward.

By the time they reached Woodhurst, Mandy was feeling more confident. Quince trotted calmly down the main street, her antlers glittering in the moonlight. Mandy was aware of smiling faces appearing in the windows of the cottages, and a few people stepped out of the inn and waved cheery Christmas greetings as they passed. And all the while, she could hear strains of "Ding, Dong, Merrily on High" floating toward them on the breeze. Surely nothing could be more Christmassy than this.

That night, Mandy dreamed of galloping ponies. Wild and beautiful, the ponies swirled around her, and the air was full of the swish of their tails and the drumming of their hooves. The drumming seemed to be getting louder. There were shouts, too — Great-Aunt Pip's voice, and Lizzie's. . . .

Mandy sat upright in bed and blinked. The drumming sound intensified, and so did the voices. In a flash, she realized that she hadn't been dreaming at all.

She ran to the window and stared out. To her astonishment, about fifteen ponies were milling around beneath her in the dull gray light of early morning, their noses in Great-Aunt Pip's vegetable garden and their hooves trampling the currant bushes. She saw Lizzie trying to coax two excitable ponies toward the gate, while her great-aunt was trying to pull Willow out of a tangle of raspberry canes. Jingle was frisking around the perimeter of the yard, kicking his legs and nimbly dodging any attempts to catch him.

"Lizzie!" Mandy exclaimed in awe as she opened the window. "Great-Aunt Pip! What's happening?"

Great-Aunt Pip looked up. "Mandy, get down here quickly!" she said. "We need your help — these ponies are wrecking my yard!"

Mandy raced down the stairs, pulling a sweater over her head and buttoning her jeans at the same time. She automatically jumped over Pyramus's step, although the cat wasn't sitting there. Then she grabbed the first pair of boots she could see, shoved her arms into a coat that was much too big for her, and rushed out the door.

There were ponies everywhere.

"What are they all *doing* here?" Mandy shouted, trying to steer a tubby little pony away from the flower beds. "And where are Mom and Dad?"

"My dad got a call about a sick pony first thing this morning," Lizzie said. She was holding Willow steady as Great-Aunt Pip carefully unwound her mane from the stubborn raspberry canes. "He asked your parents to help, so they've driven to Woodhurst."

"Do the ponies get into people's yards a lot?" Mandy asked, puffing and grabbing hold of the tubby pony's mane and trying to haul him toward the gate. The pony snorted in disapproval, shook Mandy's hand off, and trotted back to the rosebushes.

"It's quite common in the Forest." Great-Aunt Pip sighed, finally detaching Willow, who promptly pulled away from her and headed for the apple tree. "Though Willow's never brought her herd into my yard before. Where their leader goes, the rest tend to follow."

The wild ponies refused to be caught. Mandy and the others were hopelessly outnumbered. It was beginning to look like an impossible task when Quince suddenly whinnied from the Savages' field next door.

"Don't you start!" Mandy groaned as several ponies trotted over to talk to the little bay mare. Suddenly, something clicked in Mandy's mind.

"Lizzie!" she called. "Could Willow's herd have gotten into the yard because they were interested in your ponies? You just moved them into this field, right?"

Lizzie looked around from the apple tree, where Jingle was reaching into the branches and munching happily on whatever leaves he could reach. "Maybe," she said. "Why?"

Great-Aunt Pip wiped her forehead. "I don't think it

matters *why* they're here, Mandy. We just need to get them out!"

"I have an idea," Mandy said. "If Willow's herd came to see Quince and the others, maybe we can do something about it. Lizzie, could we saddle up Quince and Piper?"

Lizzie understood in a flash. "No time for saddles," she said. "The garden will be totally flattened before we've even tightened the girths. We could put bridles on them, if you're OK with riding bareback."

"No problem," Mandy said firmly. "Don't worry," she explained to her frazzled great-aunt. "The wild ponies will follow us. I'm sure of it!"

Lizzie's ponies had begun to gallop around the pasture, tossing their heads and whinnying. The excitement of the wild herd in the yard was catching. Lizzie flung a bridle at Mandy, and they both ran toward the ponies, calling them.

Quince was the first to slow down. Mandy managed to grab a handful of her chocolate brown mane and slip the bridle over her ears. Puffin was still tearing around the field. Coaxing the bit into Quince's mouth, Mandy saw that Lizzie had cornered Piper near the gate and was talking softly to him. When the skewbald finally quieted down, Lizzie put on the bridle, wrapped her hand around the pony's mane, and vaulted deftly onto his brown-and-white back.

Copying Lizzie's technique, Mandy did the same. Quince's back was warm and a bit scratchy. It seemed strange to be sitting on a pony with no saddle, and her legs felt heavy and peculiar without the security of the stirrups.

"Come on!" Lizzie called, digging her heels into Piper's sides.

Mandy pressed her knees against Quince's shoulders as tightly as she could and tried to keep her balance as the pony trotted out of the field after her companion.

Almost immediately, the wild ponies looked up.

"Open the gate as wide as you can, Pip!" Mandy called. She deliberately steered Quince toward the yard until she was sure she had the whole herd's attention, then yelled *"Go!"*

The little mare leaped forward at a flat-out gallop. Mandy leaned down close to Quince's warm neck and turned her toward the trees.

"They're coming!" Lizzie shouted, tearing after her on Piper.

Like a tide of brown, gray, black, and white, the wild ponies streamed out of Great-Aunt Pip's garden and followed Mandy and Lizzie. Mandy pressed her heels harder into Quince's flanks and she sped up so quickly that for a terrible moment Mandy thought she was going to fall off. She twisted her hands into Quince's mane and pulled herself straight again. Ponies jostled on either side of them, sending clumps of earth and mud flying up into the air. Soon the drumming of hooves was so loud that Mandy couldn't even hear herself think. Shaggy flanks pressed up against her legs, and tails and manes lashed at her knees as the herd galloped beside them.

Mandy couldn't help shouting with exhilaration. She was running with a herd of wild ponies!

"Let's pull up here!" Lizzie called at last as the trees widened out to a patch of open grassland.

Mandy heaved on the reins, wondering nervously if Quince would want to stop galloping. To her relief, Quince slowed down at once. Gradually, the rest of Willow's herd slowed down as well, snorting and blowing, before bending their heads to crop the grass. Mandy ran her hand down Quince's neck and relaxed, breathing in her warm horse smell.

"Pretty good work," Lizzie grinned at her. "For a grockle!"

After a few minutes' rest, they turned their ponies back toward Beech End Cottage. Mandy glanced back at the wild ponies, who were grazing quietly, as if nothing had happened. Jingle looked up and whinnied at her. Mandy wondered if she'd see him again before they left. *Don't be silly*, she scolded herself. *You just rode*

*with his herd! What better way to leave Jingle than
that?* Feeling a little better, she followed Lizzie onto the
pathway.

The temperature had dropped again, and the yellowish
clouds were gathering thickly overhead. Mandy shivered and tucked her hands deep inside her coat.

"Hey!" Lizzie exclaimed. "I just saw a snowflake!"

Sure enough, tiny white puffs of snow were drifting
out of the leaden sky. They swirled around Mandy and
Lizzie, falling to the ground and melting almost immediately. But soon the flakes were staying where they fell,
and the path began to resemble a ruffled chocolate cake
covered with a thin dusting of icing sugar.

"It's getting thicker," said Mandy, urging Quince into
a trot. "Let's get back."

Lizzie's eyes shone with excitement. "It's Christmas
Day tomorrow. I've never had a white Christmas! Do
you think we'll get much more snow?"

As if in answer to her question, there was a sudden
surge of white and the snow began to fall heavily.
Fortunately, Beech End Cottage was only five minutes
away. Laughing and gasping with the cold, Mandy and
Lizzie cantered the ponies back into the field, took off
their bridles, and gave them a good rubdown and a pair
of waterproof blankets to keep them warm. Lizzie
explained that usually New Forest ponies had thick

enough coats for cold weather, but she thought Quince and Piper might object to being covered in snow!

Great-Aunt Pip was standing by the gate when they made their way to Beech End Cottage. "Oh, I'm so glad you're back!" she exclaimed. "I was worried."

"The snow's not that thick!" Mandy joked.

"It's not the snow I'm worried about," Great-Aunt Pip said. "It's Pyramus. He's disappeared!"

Eight

"Disappeared?" Mandy echoed. With a sick feeling, she remembered that Pyramus hadn't been on his usual step that morning. How could she have forgotten about him? Her parents had diagnosed the gray cat as possibly having pneumonia. The cold, and now the snow, could do him serious harm if he went outside.

"I feel terrible!" Great-Aunt Pip sniffed. "In all the excitement of the ponies, I left the door open. He can't go outside in this weather!"

"It's not your fault," Mandy tried to reassure her great-aunt. "Don't worry, he won't be far away. We'll check the yard first. If he's out here, we'll get him inside as quickly as we can."

The snow was falling more and more thickly, which didn't help. Mandy hunted along the hedge, calling for Pyramus, snowflakes falling around her head and sneaking down the neck of her coat. She wished her parents would come back. They'd know where to look.

Impatiently brushing the flakes away, Mandy forced herself to think logically, the way her mom and dad did when they were trying to diagnose a sick animal. She searched inch by inch, checking the ground for footprints, cat hairs, anything that might give them a clue. *Where would a sick cat go?* she wondered. *Come on, Mandy — think!*

Lizzie approached, looking serious. Mandy's heart lurched.

"Did you find him?" she asked, dreading the answer.

But Lizzie shook her head. "I don't think he's in the yard," she said. Shading her eyes from the falling snow, she stared at the woodland around them. "He might have gotten out of the gate and gone into the Forest."

Great-Aunt Pip hurried over. "Into the Forest?" She gasped. "Pyramus sometimes goes out to hunt in the trees, but in this snow and being so sick, he may not be able to find his way home."

Be logical. Staring out at the whitening trees, Mandy couldn't believe Pyramus would have left Beech End Cottage. "He was feeling too sick to go far," she said. "Did you search inside?"

"Of course I did," said Great-Aunt Pip, sounding desperate. "In all his usual places. There was no sign of him."

"What about any *un*usual places?" Mandy suggested, heading back toward the house. "When cats get sick they like to hide in small spaces."

"Really? Why?" Lizzie was following Mandy up the path.

"It's probably a habit left over from their wild ancestors," Mandy said. "Like the way Puffin can't resist running with the herd. When wild cats get sick, they are vulnerable to being attacked. Small spaces are easier to defend."

"That makes sense," Great-Aunt Pip said. "Well, the cottage has plenty of nooks and crannies, and two fresh pairs of eyes might find something that I missed. You girls look upstairs. I'll check the kitchen and living room again."

They stepped into the hallway and brushed the snow from their shoulders. The cottage felt warm and welcoming after the bitter wind outside. Even Twit and his friends looked pleased to see them.

"Phew," Lizzie said, wrinkling her nose. "Where's that smell coming from?"

"One of your mom's candles," Mandy said, pulling off her coat and draping it on a peg by the door. She looked curiously at Lizzie, who had started coughing. "It's not that strong, is it?"

Lizzie waved her hand in front of her face. "My nose is very sensitive," she admitted. "My grandma bought me some perfume for Christmas last year. I took one whiff and couldn't stop coughing."

"I'm sure Great-Aunt Pip won't mind if we blow it out," Mandy said, bending down to the little green candle on the hall table and blowing out the flame. A trail of smoke spiraled toward the dark ceiling.

"Thanks," Lizzie said. "Let's go upstairs. It won't smell so strong up there."

There were only three rooms to search. Mandy hunted in her parents' room while Lizzie searched in Great-Aunt Pip's cupboards, calling Pyramus's name the whole time.

"If he's not in your room, Mandy, I don't think he can be upstairs at all," Lizzie said as they went into the little blue bedroom and glanced around.

Mandy started pulling clothes and bedding out of the closet behind the door while Lizzie looked underneath the bed.

"I don't see how Pyramus could have gotten into this closet, anyway," Mandy said, surveying the pile of clothes on the floor. "The door was closed. Anything under the bed?"

"Besides your old socks?" Lizzie grinned, standing up. "No — just your suitcase."

Mandy peered underneath the bed. She could see her suitcase just where she had left it, but there was no sign of anything else. She was about to wriggle out again when she noticed that the lid of the case was slightly raised. She frowned. Could a sick and frightened cat have crawled through the narrow gap?

"Pyramus?" she whispered, lifting the lid as far as she could in the cramped space. "Are you in there?"

A pair of round yellow eyes blinked at her from the shadows.

"You are!" Mandy exclaimed with relief. "Oh, Pyramus, are we glad to see you!"

She slid the suitcase out from its hiding place and opened it up. Then she gently lifted the cat out. Almost immediately, Pyramus started coughing.

"He sounds like you," Mandy said to Lizzie as she cradled the gray cat and stroked his head.

"Maybe he doesn't like strong smells, either," Lizzie joked, tickling Pyramus under the chin.

Mandy was very thoughtful as they walked back

down the narrow staircase toward the hall. Halfway down, Pyramus started coughing again. Mandy stopped, one foot hovering indecisively over the next step.

"Aren't you coming down?" Lizzie said in surprise, looking over her shoulder.

"Can you still smell the candles?" Mandy asked.

Lizzie nodded. "It's still pretty strong," she said. "Why?"

"I know this might sound crazy," Mandy said, "but what if Pyramus is reacting to the candles? What if he

really *is* like you and is allergic to strong smells?" She thought back over the past few days. Pyramus had first started acting strangely the day that Lizzie had brought the candles. It all made sense.

Lizzie stared at her. "Do cats get reactions like that?"

Mandy started walking back up the stairs, carrying Pyramus away from the scented hallway. "Tell Great-Aunt Pip to put all the candles outside!" she called down to Lizzie. "And open the windows and doors."

"But it's freezing outside!" Lizzie objected. "I thought we were supposed to keep Pyramus warm?"

"It's only for a few minutes," Mandy replied. "Just to air out the house. Pyramus and I will stay up here. And if he really is allergic to the candles, then he doesn't have a chest infection after all, and the cold won't be so dangerous."

She walked back into her room and sat down on the bed, hugging Pyramus close. "You poor thing," she whispered while the little gray cat started a feeble purr. "Don't worry. If I'm right, you'll be better in no time."

Ten minutes later, Mandy heard her dad's voice floating up from the hallway.

"It's like an icebox in here! Why are all the doors and windows wide open?"

Mandy ran to the top of the stairs with Pyramus, who

was tightly wrapped in one of her sweaters. She wasn't confident enough about her diagnosis that she was going to risk him catching a chill. Thanks to Lizzie opening the windows, the air in the cottage now smelled fresh and cool, with only the faintest hint of pine.

Great-Aunt Pip came out of the living room, wearing her thickest sweater and a wool scarf. She looked almost as wrapped up as Pyramus. "Mandy has had an idea about Pyramus," she told Dr. Adam.

"I think he's allergic to the candles," Mandy said, hurrying down the stairs with her precious bundle.

"Allergic?" Dr. Adam echoed. "Well, it's possible, I suppose — the coughing, the shallow breathing. What gave you the idea?"

Mandy explained as quickly as she could. "Great-Aunt Pip's put the candles out in the shed. Don't you think it makes sense?" she said, looking hopefully at her dad.

Dr. Adam looked impressed. "That's a very clever diagnosis, Mandy," he said, taking Pyramus from Mandy's arms and carrying him into the kitchen, which was still warm and cozy because of the stove. "Let's have a look at this guy."

Great-Aunt Pip went around the house shutting all the windows as Dr. Adam checked Pyramus over, looking in his eyes and his mouth and taking his temperature. Pyramus rolled onto his back and even managed a brief purr when Dr. Adam ran his hands up and down his chest and stomach.

At last, Dr. Adam straightened up. "Well, the fact that his temperature is normal and his reaction to the fresh air both suggest that Mandy is right, and Pyramus doesn't have any sort of infection," he announced. "His breathing is noticeably better, and his eyes look a little brighter as well."

"But what about the temperature he had a couple of days ago?" Mandy pointed out. "And he's so thin. Does that happen with allergies?"

Dr. Adam thoughtfully stroked his beard. "It's possible that Pyramus had a temperature the other day because he'd been sitting too close to the fire," he suggested. "As for the weight loss, I noticed just now that his teeth need filing. Perhaps he's been having trouble eating because of that. Have you changed his food recently, Pip?"

"Yes, I have," Great-Aunt Pip said, nodding. "They'd run out of his usual kind in Woodhurst."

"I suggest you get him back on his old food again," Dr. Adam advised. "And ask your vet to take care of his teeth. That'll make him more comfortable when he chews. As for the allergic reaction, if that's what it is, a dose of antihistamine should do the trick."

Great-Aunt Pip beamed. "You'll be a fully qualified vet

before you know it, Mandy," she said as Dr. Adam prepared the antihistamine injection.

"I hope so," Mandy said with a grin. "But it's all thanks to Lizzie, really. If she hadn't coughed, I wouldn't have figured it out." She looked around. "Where is Lizzie, anyway?"

"She had to go home," said Great-Aunt Pip, lifting Pyramus off the table and settling him down by the stove. "But I've invited the Savages over for supper, so you'll see her later."

"I'll cook," Dr. Adam offered promptly.

"What are you going to make?" Mandy asked, her mouth watering as she thought about her dad's legendary cauliflower cheese dish, made with extra cream and four different cheeses.

"Something light, I think," Dr. Adam decided, dashing Mandy's hopes. "So we can fit in all that food tomorrow." He patted his stomach. "I want plenty of space in here for the turkey!"

Mandy's dad buried his nose in Great-Aunt Pip's cookbooks after offering to cook supper. Mandy had a sneaking suspicion that he was remembering Tim Savage's perfect mince tarts and was determined to give Great-Aunt Pip's neighbors a meal to remember. Great-Aunt Pip made thick cheese-and-tomato sandwiches for a late lunch, and Mandy wolfed them down in case tonight's supper was a little *too* light.

After twenty minutes, Dr. Adam announced that he'd found the perfect recipe: a risotto made with roasted peppers. Then he called Mandy's mom, who was still out shopping, so that she could pick up the ingredients from the supermarket on her way back.

"Good thing you called me," Dr. Emily said an hour later, as Mandy helped her unpack the grocery bags. "The snow started coming down so hard when I turned off the road, I could hardly see the house. I wouldn't like to go out in it now."

Mandy pressed her nose to the kitchen window and watched the flakes swirling in the evening darkness. She was mesmerized by the way they steadily piled up on the sill. Peering beyond the white yard, she could just make out the outline of Quince, Piper, and Puffin huddled in the middle of the Savages' field. They looked very glad to have on their winter blankets. "What will the wild ponies do in this weather?" she asked, suddenly feeling worried.

"Find a cozy, sheltered spot, I guess," said her mom, putting the last of the groceries in the fridge. "There are plenty of thick holly bushes in the forest to protect them from the wind. It's the wind that does the damage, you know, not the snow itself. Don't worry about them,

Mandy. Those thick coats of theirs will keep them dry. Now, this is the kind of weather for roasting chestnuts on an open fire, don't you think?" She produced a bag of shiny brown chestnuts from the last shopping bag and swung them tantalizingly. "Let's stoke up the fire and put the kettle on in the living room!"

The snow fell steadily all afternoon as Mandy, her parents, and her great-aunt sat in front of the fire and played cards. Already looking much happier, Pyramus sat on a cushion next to the fire and purred loudly. Soon, all that could be seen of Great-Aunt Pip's yard out of the living room window was a series of white bumps and lumps. The currant bushes slowly disappeared under a coat of snow, and the vegetable garden vanished completely, except for a faint dimpled outline. Staring out the window, Mandy peeled a warm chestnut and popped the sweet, floury-tasting nut into her mouth.

"I hope you've left some room for supper," her dad warned, checking his watch. "I'm going to start making it. The Savages will be here in an hour."

Mandy thought about her dad's plans for a light meal that evening and picked up another chestnut — just to be on the safe side. She followed her dad into the kitchen. "Do you need any help?"

Her dad had her chop peppers and onions, and soon the kitchen was filled with the sweet smell of roasting vegetables. A large pot of water was put on the stove to boil, and Mandy hunted through Great-Aunt Pip's kitchen drawers for a lively red tablecloth. After all, it was Christmas Eve! She wanted the supper to be as festive as possible. As she put the finishing touch on the table — a bunch of prickly holly smothered in red berries — she glanced up to see her dad frowning, a wooden spoon in his hand.

"This sauce is missing something," he said, offering the spoon to Mandy. "What do you think?"

"It's delicious," Mandy told him, handing the spoon back.

Dr. Adam reached for the fridge anyway, and pulled out a carton of cream. "Just a dollop," he said as Mandy raised her eyebrows.

"I thought this was going to be a light meal!" Mandy said, laughing.

Dr. Adam poured in a second dollop of cream. "Well," he said, his eyes twinkling. "Lightish."

Mandy was chopping the last of the parsley for the garnish when the doorbell rang. She went to answer it and showed everyone into the kitchen. Soon the room was filled with laughter and conversation. Mandy ate as much risotto as she could, wishing she hadn't eaten quite as many chestnuts that afternoon.

"Apple crumble for dessert," announced Great-Aunt Pip, pulling a dish from the oven and placing it on the table. "But I'm afraid I can't find the cream, so I hope it'll be OK on its own."

Mandy caught her dad's eye and tried not to laugh as everyone helped themselves. Suddenly, the doorbell rang shrilly. It was so unexpected that they all stopped talking and put down their spoons.

"Who can that be?" Great-Aunt Pip wondered out loud.

"I'll get it," Mandy offered. She pushed back her chair and hurried into the hall. Through the pane of glass in the front door, she could see the outline of someone in a large overcoat.

"Is the Agister here?" said their visitor when she opened the door. The man was wringing his hands and looked terribly upset.

Tim Savage came into the hallway. "I'm the Agister," he said. "What happened?"

"I was driving along the road just now," the man said, gesturing behind him, "and I skidded on a patch of ice, right onto the shoulder of the road. There was nothing I could do." He stopped and swallowed. "I'm afraid I hit a pony."

Nine

The taste of apple crumble turned to sawdust in Mandy's mouth.

"Where did this happen?" Mr. Savage demanded, reaching for his coat.

The man looked even more miserable. "Not far along the road to Lymington," he said. "The pony looked badly hurt. I stopped at your house but when you weren't at home, I guessed you hadn't gone far in this weather. Sorry to interrupt your evening."

"You did the right thing," Mr. Savage said. He glanced over his shoulder to where everyone was gathered by the kitchen door. "Sorry, Pip. I've got to go."

"Of course," said Great-Aunt Pip, nodding.

"We'll come with you," said Dr. Adam, while Mandy's mom reached for the vet's bag.

Still standing beside the door, Mandy found that she couldn't move her feet. "What did the pony look like?" she whispered.

"It was gray," the man replied. "There was a young one, too, but I don't think I hit him. He ran off."

"Willow!" Lizzie screamed, pushing past her parents. "It's Willow!"

All thoughts of the meal were forgotten as everyone ran out of the house.

Mr. Savage borrowed a storm lantern from Great-Aunt Pip, and it spread a warm yellow light through the falling snow. It was hard to see where they were going; the snow blew around their faces, disorienting them, while the road and the trees looked strange and different in their snowy white coats.

Tears rolled down Lizzie's cheeks as she and Mandy followed the others. Mandy could hear her parents talking together in low, grave voices — they obviously feared the worst for the poor pony.

"Maybe it's not Willow." Mandy tried to stop her voice from wobbling.

"I know it is." Lizzie wept. "Here, in my heart. You know it, too, don't you?"

Ahead of them, the others had stopped to gather around a still, gray shape lying on the roadside. In the silence, Mandy felt her heart break in two as she recognized the motionless pony. Beside her, Lizzie moaned.

Dr. Adam knelt down and very gently rested his hand on Willow's neck. Snow fell softly around her, piling against her flanks in little drifts. Mandy could see that Willow was still breathing, but only just. She bit hard on her lip when she saw a small trickle of blood seeping out of Willow's nose. That was the worst possible sign.

"It looks as if she has a badly broken leg, several broken ribs, and some severe internal injuries," Dr. Adam said sadly as he ran his hands over Willow's side. He looked up at them. "I'm sorry, but it's too late to help her. The best thing we can do is put her out of pain."

"No!" Lizzie burst out. "She's still breathing! There must be something you can do!"

Mandy's mom gazed at her with compassion in her eyes. "The snow must have muffled the sound of the car and taken Willow by surprise. The car went right off the road, and she didn't have a chance. The kindest thing is to end her pain, Lizzie," she said. "I'm so sorry it has to be this way."

"No! Dad, tell them!" Sobbing, Lizzie fell on her knees in the snow.

"It's OK, Lizzie," Mr. Savage said gently, leaning down to help his daughter to her feet. "It's for the best. Mandy will take care of you. Come away, please."

Mandy swallowed her own tears and put her arm around Lizzie's shoulders. However much her heart was breaking for poor, brave Willow, it must be a hundred times worse for Lizzie, who had known the mare so much longer. She led her friend away from the scene, glad that the falling snow would cloak the grim sound of the bolt gun.

Beneath the snow-laden trees, the air was so still that Mandy could hear the painful beat of her heart. Lizzie hid her face in her hands, pulling away from Mandy. "Go away!" she cried, her voice thick with tears. "Leave me alone!"

Mandy laid a hand on her shoulder. "Willow's gone, Lizzie," she said. "We can't do anything for her now."

"But what about Jingle?" Lizzie sobbed. "He's lost his mom."

Jingle! Mandy's heart twisted. Where was he? The driver said he'd only hit one pony, but in this weather, with so much snow, how could he be sure?

She took Lizzie by the shoulders. "We have to find Jingle," she said urgently. "That's something we can do for Willow. Find her colt, and make sure he's OK."

Lizzie sniffed and wiped her nose on her sleeve. "Find

Jingle," she echoed, hiccupping. "Yes, you're right. But where do we look?"

Mandy glanced around. The snow was changing everything, piling high on branches and turning their footprints into indistinct dimples. There was no hope of following Jingle's tracks in this weather. They just had to hope that the colt hadn't gone far.

"Stay here," she instructed. "I'm going to tell Mom what we're doing. I'll borrow her cell phone so we can call her if we find Jingle and we need help. Then we can start looking."

She ran back to her parents, trying not to look at the unmoving gray shape on the road. "Looking for Jingle might take Lizzie's mind off Willow," she explained. "If he's hurt, we can call you."

"Good thinking," said her mom, pressing a flashlight and her phone into Mandy's hand. "We're going to head back and get Tim's truck so we can get Willow off the road. If you need help with Jingle, just let us know. Don't get cold, and don't stay out too long. Half an hour max, OK? Then I want you back at Beech End Cottage. Nothing can help Willow now, and freezing to death won't do Jingle any good, either. Understand?"

"Jingle will be all right, won't he?" Lizzie whispered when Mandy returned. "That driver said he only hit one pony, not two."

Mandy crossed her fingers inside her mittens. "I'm sure he'll be fine," she said encouragingly.

They set out into the forest, calling Jingle's name and peering through tangled white undergrowth to search for tracks. Mandy saw the prints of foxes and squirrels and neat little bird footprints that hardly dented the ground, but everything was quickly disappearing as the snow fell relentlessly. It was impossible to tell if Jingle's prints were among the dimples on the white ground. Mandy shivered. The forest was spooky at night, especially with the muffling effect of the snow. Holding the torch as steadily as she could, she started singing Christmas carols to boost their spirits — anything she could think of, just as she had when she'd rescued Jingle from the bog. After a pause, Lizzie joined in. The snow deadened the sound, making their voices sound small and scared.

"This isn't working," Mandy said, sighing, after another ten minutes of wandering in circles. "What if we saddled up Quince and Piper? We'd be able to search more of the Forest."

"We'd get a better view from up on the ponies' backs, too," Lizzie agreed.

They trudged back through the snow toward Beech End Cottage and the Savages' house. Quince and Piper looked a bit surprised at being taken for a ride in the snow but allowed Mandy and Lizzie to lead them into the shelter and saddle them up. Lizzie reached up to a high shelf and pulled down a tub of grease. "Here," she said, "put this in Quince's hooves. It will stop the snow from balling up in their feet."

"How do you know that?" Mandy asked in astonishment as she lifted Quince's hooves in turn and slathered on the sticky grease. "I thought you'd never seen snow before."

Lizzie gave a wan smile. "I read about it once," she said. "I can't believe I'm trying it out for real."

The view from the ponies' backs was very different, and Mandy found that she could see much farther among the trees with the flashlight. Sitting astride Quince's warm back was comforting, and Mandy felt safer out in the strange white woodland. Thanks to Lizzie's sense of direction and knowledge of the Forest, they followed familiar trails made unfamiliar by the snow. Several times they passed huddles of wild ponies sheltering beneath the trees. But Jingle wasn't among them.

"Shh!" Mandy pulled Quince to a standstill. "I think I heard something, over there." She pointed to a thicket of hazel trees, their branches drooping under the weight of snow.

There was a crack, as if something heavy had stepped on a twig. Mandy and Lizzie peered across the snowy glade and heard the unmistakable sound of a loudly breathing pony. If it was one pony on its own, it was probably Jingle, because all the other Forest ponies would stick close to their herds in this weather.

"Don't scare him," Lizzie cautioned as they dismounted and crept toward the thicket.

"Jingle!" Mandy used her most soothing voice and angled the flashlight upward so that it didn't dazzle the pony. "It's us, boy. We've come to rescue you."

There was a rustle and a nervous whinny, followed by another snap of twigs underfoot. They saw a pale roan nose emerging from the thicket, followed moments later by Jingle himself. The young colt was breathing heavily, his flanks damp with sweat. He tossed his head up and down and his eyes rolled timidly as he pawed at the ground. He looked ready to bolt at any moment.

"He doesn't look hurt," Lizzie whispered.

Mandy didn't want to point out that shock could be as dangerous for the young pony as a physical injury. She reached her hand toward the shivering colt. "It's OK, boy," she murmured. "Remember me? You can trust me. I saved you before, and I'm going to save you again."

Jingle took one trembling step toward her, then

another. Then, with a sigh, the colt quietly laid his chin on Mandy's shoulder.

"Call my dad, Lizzie," Mandy whispered, passing across her mom's phone with one hand and reaching up to rest the other on Jingle's nose. "We need to get him somewhere warm — and fast."

Ten long minutes later, the girls' parents rolled up in Mr. Savage's Land Rover with a trailer rattling behind. Mandy coaxed Jingle toward the vehicle, praying that he wouldn't lash out and run away. To her relief, the colt followed her meekly, his head hanging low. It was as if he'd given up trying to fight and didn't care what happened anymore.

"Steady there, boy," Dr. Adam murmured, helping Mandy to encourage the young colt up the ramp. Almost as if he were sleepwalking, Jingle stumbled into the trailer.

"Do you want me to put a halter on him and tie him up?" Mandy offered.

Mr. Savage shook his head. "He's never been in a trailer before or worn a halter. I think tying him up will just scare him more. We'll leave him loose and drive as carefully as we can."

"Pip is preparing a stall for him," Dr. Emily said,

opening the car door for Mandy and Lizzie. "We'll give him some hot mash and keep him warm, then look at him more closely in the morning."

If he lasts the night. With a heavy heart, Mandy heard her mother's unspoken words. Jingle had seen his mother killed by a car and nearly been killed himself. A shock like that could be fatal. There was very little they could do unless Jingle chose to fight back. And judging from the way he could barely stand, he was in no mood to fight anything.

They drove back in silence. There was a light on in the little stable behind Beech End Cottage, and Mandy could see Great-Aunt Pip carrying armfuls of what looked like ferns across the yard. They lowered the ramp and Mandy put her arm around Jingle's neck to guide him into the stall. Even though he had lived outdoors all his life, the colt didn't seem interested in exploring this strange new place. Instead, he stood stiff-legged, with his head hanging so low that his muzzle almost rested on the floor.

Lizzie began brushing him with a twist of straw, rubbing his damp coat in soothing, rhythmical circles before draping him in one of Piper's blankets. It was far too big, even with the buckles on the tightest holes, and hung down to Jingle's knees in a way that might have looked adorable if Mandy hasn't been so desperately worried about him.

"Is he going to be OK, Dad?" she asked.

"Hard to say," Dr. Adam admitted, taking out his stethoscope to listen to the colt's chest. "His heart is racing and his breathing is very shallow. There's a gallon of adrenaline charging through his system that could act as a poison. It's really up to Jingle now."

Mandy stroked Jingle's nose. "Did you hear that?" she told him, fighting to keep her voice steady. "It's all up to you, you brave and beautiful pony."

"Help me spread this on the floor, Mandy," Great-Aunt Pip said, handing her a mound of dry brown ferns, which she called bracken. "And tuck some of it under Jingle's rug. It's a great way of insulating him from the cold."

"Don't you have any straw?" Mandy asked, stuffing handfuls of bracken underneath Jingle's blanket.

"Why buy straw when we can collect bracken for free?" Great-Aunt Pip gave a gentle smile. "It's an old Forest tradition, stretching back almost a thousand years."

The bracken was cool and wood scented, like the Forest itself on a bright autumn day. If anything could soothe Jingle, it would be this — the smell of home.

"Can we stay in the stable with Jingle tonight?" Mandy turned and looked pleadingly at her parents.

"Oh, yes," Lizzie begged. "We'll be able to look after him all night and call you if there's anything wrong."

"Are you sure?" Dr. Emily poured some hot bran mash into the manger. "It won't be very comfortable."

"If it's comfy enough for Jingle, it's comfy enough for us," Mandy declared. "Great-Aunt Pip, do you have a space heater we can borrow? We'll bring in more blankets, and hot water bottles —"

"We can put hot water bottles on Jingle's legs," Lizzie added. "It's great for helping circulation."

"Yes, and we can talk to him!" Mandy finished. "Talking is good for shock."

"OK." Dr. Emily nodded. "Anything that might help Jingle would be good, although you must be prepared for the worst. This really could go either way."

Mandy swallowed and glanced at Lizzie. Her mother was right, but it was still very hard to accept.

"Just keep warm, OK?" Dr. Emily continued with a sympathetic smile. "I don't want to come out on Christmas morning and find you've turned into a pair of icicles."

Mandy and Lizzie gathered as many pillows and blankets as they could find, while Great-Aunt Pip supplied four hot water bottles and a kettle. Mr. Savage brought some warm clothes for Lizzie and a small electric heater that quickly warmed the chilly, bracken-scented stable.

Mandy put on every pair of socks she could find, and Lizzie loaned her a soft wool hat. Then they plugged any drafty gaps around the door and windows with more handfuls of bracken and curled up next to Jingle. The pony was lying down now, stretched out with his head flat on the floor. He looked comfortable but his breathing seemed very shallow, which made Mandy anxious.

"We should take turns watching him," she suggested to Lizzie, setting the alarm on her watch. "I'll do the first couple of hours. You get some sleep."

While Lizzie settled down among the blankets, Mandy tried to coax Jingle into eating some of the rapidly cooling mash, talking gently all the while. She boiled the kettle and added more hot water to the bran, but Jingle just sighed and closed his eyes.

She vaguely remembered that it was Christmas Eve. Normally, she'd be really excited by now, hanging up her stocking, wrapping last-minute presents, and getting ready for midnight Mass. But those things seemed very far away tonight. Bowing her head, Mandy laid her hand on Jingle's neck and tried to send strong, positive thoughts through her fingertips instead. *Get well, be strong, get well, be strong. . . .*

"I'll refill the hot water bottles," Lizzie said, yawning, when Mandy wearily shook her awake two hours later. "Don't worry, Mandy. I'll wake you if anything happens."

Gratefully, Mandy snuggled down in the bracken and closed her eyes.

It seemed only moments later when she felt Lizzie's hand on her shoulder. Opening her eyes, Mandy found herself looking at four roan-colored legs standing unsteadily beside her. Glancing up, she saw Jingle burying his nose in the manger.

"He's eating!" She gasped and scrambled to her feet. "He's going to be OK!"

"I knew Jingle wouldn't give in without a fight." Lizzie grinned and looked down at her watch. "It's midnight, Mandy. Merry Christmas!"

Ten

Something was tickling Mandy's cheek. Pushing it away, she tried to go back to the dream she'd been having — all about Jingle, and meadows, and warm sunshine. But the tickling returned. She reluctantly opened her eyes and saw Lizzie smiling down at her, holding a little piece of bracken in her hand.

"Wake up!" she said, tickling Mandy on the nose. "It's Christmas Day!"

Mandy was suddenly aware of a warm velvety nose nuzzling at her neck. "Merry Christmas, Jingle," she said, and laughed. Jingle whickered softly at her, his big brown eyes bright and friendly.

"You have to come and see this, Mandy," Lizzie called, peering out the window. "It's the most beautiful thing I've ever seen."

It was like looking out at a Christmas card. It had stopped snowing, and on every tree the branches hung low, weighed down with glittering snowflakes. Above, the sky was a piercing blue.

There was a crunching sound outside and Dr. Adam, wearing a bright red hat and humming a carol, appeared with a tray in his hands.

"Breakfast!" Mandy sighed happily, running to open the stable door. "I'm starving!"

"Merry Christmas!" said her dad, setting the tray down on a straw bale. "I've brought tea, muffins, scrambled eggs, and two stockings from Santa Claus for you, too. It's past eleven o'clock — you've already missed the Christmas service. We let you sleep, since you were probably up half the night."

"Did you come in earlier to give Jingle his breakfast?" Lizzie asked, cradling the mug of hot tea.

"I came out at six to check on him," Dr. Adam said, nodding. "You obviously worked wonders on him in the night. I gave him his mash as quietly as I could so I wouldn't wake you. But there wasn't much chance of that. You were both out cold!"

He pulled a radio out of his pocket and set it down on

the windowsill. Soon the sound of Christmas carols filled the stable.

"Oh, wow!" Lizzie exclaimed, pulling a new grooming brush from her stocking. "This is great! Mine's totally worn out."

Mandy found a cuddly gray toy cat in her stocking that reminded her of Pyramus, and a pair of thermal gloves. While they ate their breakfast, the girls talked about Willow.

"It hurts every time I think of her," Lizzie admitted. "But at least we saved Jingle."

"And since he's already weaned, he can stay with his herd," Mandy pointed out.

They both looked at Jingle, who was watching them from the other side of the stable.

"I'm going to try my new brush on him right now," Lizzie declared, finishing her last bite of muffin. "I'm going to make that fluffy little coat of his shine like nothing else!"

Mandy and Lizzie stayed in the stable for the rest of the morning, taking turns brushing Jingle's coat and combing his mane and tail. Jingle seemed delighted with all the attention and nibbled affectionately on Mandy's sleeve whenever he could reach her. Mandy knew that if Willow were still alive, she'd be the one comforting her colt after his terrifying night. She and Lizzie weren't the same, but Mandy was determined to give Jingle as much love as she could to make up for his loss. She had lost her birth parents in a car crash when she was a baby, so she and Jingle had something in common.

It was a very unusual Christmas Day, but everyone seemed to enjoy the change. Lizzie's parents came over from Clearfield Cottage with her presents, and Great-Aunt Pip bustled in and out of the stable with hot drinks. Mandy's parents brought in an awkward-shaped package for their daughter.

"It's the fox from the gallery!" Mandy gasped as she pulled back the wrapping paper and stared at the flowing wooden sculpture in astonishment. "How did you know I wanted it?"

"Helen and I got to talking at one of the rehearsals," Dr. Adam said, grinning. "She mentioned that you couldn't take your eyes off it the other day."

"Lunch is just about ready," Dr. Emily added, heading for the stable door.

"Can I bring my lunch in here, Mom?" Mandy pleaded.

Lizzie turned to her own parents. "Can I do that, too?"

"Between Jingle and all this snow, something tells me we won't be seeing much of you two today," Mr. Savage said with a smile.

*　　*　　*

After lunch, Mandy and Lizzie crunched through the snow to the ponies' field to wish Quince, Piper, and Puffin a Merry Christmas. The three ponies were huddled close together in the middle of the field.

"They know how to keep warm," Mandy said, leaning on the fence. "Brr! The worst thing about snow is how cold your feet get."

"You just need warming up," said Lizzie, a gleam of mischief in her eyes. She bent down and scooped up a handful of snow. "Bet you can't catch me!" she challenged, flinging it at Mandy.

"Bet I can!" Mandy declared, grabbing a snowball for herself and racing after Lizzie.

Back in the stable after hot baths and a change of clothes, the girls invented a card game to keep warm, which they called *Energy Snap*. It involved leaping up, jumping over a bale of straw, skipping with a piece of old rope they'd found hanging on the back of the door, kissing Jingle on the nose, and racing back every time a matching pair of cards appeared. Mandy thought she could feel Willow's comforting presence the whole time. With a sudden sense of peace, she knew that the gray mare's spirit would always be here in the Forest, watching over her herd and her colt as if she'd never left.

"Whoa!" Great-Aunt Pip exclaimed, coming into the stable just as a breathless Lizzie and Mandy were racing across the floor toward their playing cards. "If I'm not interrupting, I've brought someone else who'd like to wish you a Merry Christmas."

She unwrapped her scarf, and Pyramus's head peeped over the folds, his furry gray ears swiveling with interest.

"He's almost back to his old self," Great-Aunt Pip said fondly as Pyramus wriggled out of her grasp and pounced on a piece of bracken that was blowing across the floor. She glanced up at Jingle. "So this is Jingle by daylight, is it?" she said. "He's even more like Highfields Faraway than I thought."

"Mr. Savage said you won lots of ribbons with Highfields Faraway," Mandy said, stroking Jingle's neck and resting her face against his cheek. "That must have been wonderful."

Great-Aunt Pip's eyes grew dreamy. "Highfields Faraway was a champion of champions," she said. "And he even won the greatest prize of all — Mountain and Moorland Champion at the National Pony Show. But the thing I'll always remember him for was the December twenty-sixth point-to-point race. Straight as an arrow he went, through parts of the Forest even I didn't know. He won his race by several lengths. I hardly had to do a thing, apart from stay on his back."

"You *raced* him?" Mandy said in surprise. "I thought he was a show pony?"

"The Boxing Day point-to-point, on December twenty-sixth, is another New Forest tradition," Lizzie explained. "You'll see it tomorrow. There are about ten different races for children and adults, and there's no course — just a starting point and a finishing point. You have to cross the Forest by the quickest route you know."

Mandy laughed. "That sounds crazy!"

Great-Aunt Pip's eyes gleamed. "Crazy, but fun," she said.

Mandy turned to Lizzie. "Are you entering tomorrow?"

Lizzie shook her head. "Piper's too young," she said. "The ponies need to have seen at least four Drifts to qualify. But we always go to watch it. Dad gets a great spot near the finish line."

Mandy grinned. In spite of the pain of losing Willow, which was still like an icicle in her chest, this was turning out to be one of the most exciting Christmases ever. "I'll definitely be there!" she declared, dropping a kiss on Jingle's nose.

That evening, Jingle was given plenty of hay and mash and a bucket of tepid water. He seemed restless when Mandy went in to say good night, and he kicked at the stable door.

"Dad says we can take you back into the Forest tomorrow, if you're well enough," Mandy promised.

"You've been through so much, you beautiful pony. Now you deserve to go home and be with your friends." She swallowed hard and whispered, "Your mom will be watching over you. I know it."

She felt sad and happy at the same time as she bolted the door and trudged back to Beech End Cottage, where she ate a quick supper and then fell into bed after making her parents promise that they could go to the Boxing Day point-to-point with the Savages. It was only seven o'clock, but it felt like midnight. She fell asleep so quickly that she didn't even notice when her mom turned out the light.

The sky was grayer the next morning, and the air felt a little warmer. Mandy got up and went to the window. The Forest looked as beautiful as it had the previous day, but the snow had a soft, wet sheen that suggested it would melt away before very long.

"How's Pyramus this morning?" Mandy asked when she came downstairs. Great-Aunt Pip was at the kitchen table, making up neat little gift boxes for the postman and the milkman.

"Bright as a button," she replied, putting the finishing touches on the boxes and standing back to admire her work. "There," she said with satisfaction. "Five dollars in each box, for a happy Boxing Day."

"We don't make boxes at home," Mandy confessed. "We just give the postman a Christmas card with some money in it." Mandy instantly decided to make boxes for the Welford deliverymen next year. "Have you checked on Jingle this morning, Dad?" she asked, reaching for the orange juice. "Do you think we can let him go back into the forest?"

"He seems fine," Dr. Adam said, "just a little bored. I don't blame him. If I were a wild pony, I imagine that a stable would feel like a prison after a while. We could certainly try to set him free this morning."

There was a knock at the kitchen door.

"Morning!" Lizzie said cheerfully. "I came to see Jingle. How is he?"

"Much better," Mandy told her, rinsing her oatmeal bowl and taking a long sip of her juice. "Dad says we can take him back to the forest!"

"Great!" Lizzie exclaimed. "Dad told me he'd seen Jingle's herd close by this morning, just across the road. We can take him to them."

Dr. Adam frowned. "I don't think it's something you should attempt on your own," he said. "Jingle's a wild pony, which means he's unpredictable. I think it might be better if Tim and I handled him."

"But, Dad, he *knows* us," Mandy protested. "He won't hurt us, I'm sure of it!"

Her dad looked uncertain. "OK, as long as you promise to call me if you need help," he said at last. "You may have nursed him back to health, but ultimately he's bigger and stronger than you. Just stay away from his hooves!"

Mandy pulled on her boots and coat and ran across to the stable with Lizzie. Jingle looked pleased to see them, tossing his head and whinnying.

"Time to go home, boy!" Mandy announced. "Everything will feel better when you're back with your herd, I promise."

Cautiously, she unbolted the stall door. Jingle shook his mane, now gleaming and free of tangles since Lizzie and Mandy had brushed it so thoroughly the day before. He took a tentative step out the stable door and sniffed at the air. Lizzie took a handful of his mane and helped Mandy to lead the colt out of the stable and down toward the road.

As they approached the road, Jingle stopped. Mandy tried to coax him forward, but the colt dug his hooves in. His nostrils widened and he snorted loudly, skittering backward as a car flew past.

Mandy exchanged a worried glance with Lizzie. "Easy, boy," she soothed. "We don't have to stay on the road for long. Your herd is on the other side, waiting for you."

But Jingle wouldn't budge, laying his ears flat against

his head and rolling his eyes. He wheeled around on the gravel, dragging Mandy and Lizzie with him.

"We'll have to take him back to the stable," Mandy said, clinging onto his mane. The last thing they wanted was for Jingle to bolt under a car. "He's not ready."

"I don't blame him," Lizzie said sadly as they headed back to the stable, away from the road. Jingle seemed happy to walk beside them. "I'd never want to go near a road again if I'd seen what Jingle did."

But what does this mean for Jingle's future? Mandy wondered dismally. *What future could there be for a wild New Forest pony that was terrified by the outside world?*

"What are we going to do about Jingle?" Mandy asked Lizzie as they saddled Piper and Puffin after lunch. "Great-Aunt Pip can't keep him in her stable forever."

"We'll talk to Dad about it after the races," Lizzie promised. "Here, take some of these." She thrust a handful of flyers at Mandy. "They're about traffic awareness," she explained. "Dad wants us to pass them around the crowd at the point-to-point."

Mandy took the pages and swung herself up on Puffin's broad gray back. Then she followed Lizzie down the Forest path. They'd arranged to meet their parents and Great-Aunt Pip at the finish line later on, but Lizzie had promised to show her the starting point first.

As they rode through the Forest, Mandy was amazed at the number of people streaming through the snowy woodland. Cars were parked bumper to bumper along the roads, and the trees seemed to echo with voices and laughter. Mandy handed flyers out left and right, and most people were so willing to read them that she was encouraged, and felt they were doing something positive to prevent more accidents like Willow's. *We'll deal with the problem of Jingle later*, she decided, determined not to let her gloomy thoughts spoil the day.

"Here we are," Lizzie declared, bringing Piper to a stop at the edge of a wide stretch of heathland. "The races start over there, where the flags are."

She pointed across the heath. Several dozen ponies milled around the starting line, their riders chatting and drinking hot tea from thermoses. Each competitor wore a white waterproof vest with large black numbers on. It wasn't like a regular racecourse at all. Instead, the atmosphere reminded Mandy of a huge family party where everyone knew one another, and she felt envious and proud all at the same time.

The crack of a starting pistol burst into the air, and Mandy watched ten ponies race away across the heath, fanning out in all directions. Although Puffin snorted and tugged longingly at the reins, she managed to keep him from joining in.

"We'll go the long way to the finish," Lizzie said. "We won't catch the end of this race, but hopefully we'll see the end of the next one. Come on!"

The Forest had never seemed more beautiful to Mandy as they galloped down paths and twisted along trails, ducking to avoid snow-laden branches and jumping over logs smothered in pure, glittering layers of white.

"Whoa!" Hot and breathless, they reined in the ponies as they approached some spectators beside a row of pitched white tents. Loudspeakers were hung from the trees, and banners fluttered their support for different ponies. Mandy could see the finishing line a little way across the heath.

Sitting astride a very docile-looking Quince, Mr. Savage looked over the heads of the crowd and waved. Mandy and Lizzie rode Piper and Puffin over to where their families had gathered, five yards from the finish. Everyone was well wrapped up against the cold, and Great-Aunt Pip, wearing a large purple hat, was distributing coffee and cookies.

"Mandy, Lizzie, there you are!" she exclaimed. "We wondered when we'd see you. Terrific turnout, isn't it? Now, Lizzie, would you be a dear and get some paper towels from the refreshments tent? This awful thermos is leaking all over my coat. And, Mandy, Andrew Graves is down at the finish line and he needs some help checking entry numbers for the runners. I told him I'd send someone along."

"Still in charge, Pip!" Dr. Emily said, laughing and cradling her hot coffee.

Dr. Adam leaned on Puffin's withers and looked up at Mandy. "Before you go to help Mr. Graves," he said, "Tim has something to tell you about Jingle."

Mandy's heart plummeted into her boots. Mr. Savage was looking very serious.

"I understand that you and Lizzie had some trouble when you tried to release Jingle this morning?" he said.

All Mandy's fears about Jingle's future came crashing back. "You're not going to send him away from the Forest, are you?" she cried. "I know he's scared of the road, but there must be some way of training him to cope with his fear. He can't leave his home, not after losing his mom!"

"Hey!" Mr. Savage laughed, holding up his hands. "We're not sending him away. But it's clear that he can't return to the wild, so we've come up with a plan."

"But —" Mandy began to protest.

"Let Mr. Savage finish," her mom said gently. "You might like what he has to say."

Mr. Savage smiled. "We've decided to bring him in a little earlier than we originally planned and give him a permanent home with us. Usually, we'd leave him with his herd for a couple more years, until he's four or five, but I don't think that's what Jingle needs right now."

"If he stays with the Savages, they can give him the care he needs to help him get over losing his mom and his fear of roads," Mandy's dad explained.

"We'll have a new Highfields Faraway for the show ring, too, let's not forget!" Great-Aunt Pip declared, dabbing at her coat with the paper towels Lizzie had just brought from the refreshments tent.

"That's definitely an added bonus." Mr. Savage grinned.

"We could try grazing Jingle with Piper in the Forest field," Lizzie suggested earnestly. "It's next to the road, but he'd be safely fenced in. That would be a great way to get him used to traffic again, don't you think?"

"That's an idea!" Mandy agreed enthusiastically. All her worries about Jingle melted away. The young colt would have a home and a family, and a bright future as well. Lizzie and her family knew so much about ponies and the ways of the Forest — Jingle couldn't hope for a better life. Mandy felt as if she was about to float out of Puffin's saddle and up to the sky.

There was a sudden burst of hoofbeats as the racing

ponies burst out of the trees and dashed toward the finish line. But right now, Mandy's head was filled with thoughts of Jingle and his new home. She dropped the reins onto Puffin's neck and leaned across his withers to hug Lizzie in triumph. Puffin's head shot up as the galloping ponies approached. Too late! Mandy realized what was about to happen.

She made a grab for the reins, but Puffin had already leaped away from the others and was sprinting toward the competitors.

"Hey!" Mandy gasped as the little gray pony flew among the racing ponies. To her horror, she saw the finish line looming ahead. Somehow, she was in the race!

"Look out!"

"Hey, get out of the way!"

Riders all around her were shouting and waving their arms.

"Sorry!" Mandy shouted, desperately hauling on Puffin's reins. "This wasn't my idea."

With his neck stretched out flat like a thoroughbred's, Puffin pushed through the other ponies and bounded across the finish line. The other ponies had been galloping flat out for several minutes, whereas he had crossed the Forest more slowly, so it wasn't hard to outrun them. The other riders looked dismayed at the sight of a pony that looked as if it had hardly broken a sweat.

Puffin thundered across the finish line, then seemed to realize that he was on his own and slowed down to wait for his friends.

"Oh, no!" Mandy hid her face in her hands while Puffin tossed his head as if he'd just won the Derby. "Puffin, what have you done?"

"And we have a winner!" a voice declared from a nearby loudspeaker. "Er, the young lady seems to have lost her identification along the way. Do we have an entry number for this competitor?"